"Little did they know, they were merely disposable chess pieces in the greatest game ever played."

DOUBLECROSS

MISSION HURRICANE

THE 39 CLUES

JENNY GOEBEL

SCHOLASTIC INC.

WITHDRAWN

For Mallory Kass, with overflowing
gratitude and admiration
—J.G.

Copyright © 2016 by Scholastic Inc.

All rights reserved. Published by
Scholastic Inc., *Publishers since 1920.*
SCHOLASTIC, THE 39 CLUES, and associated logos
are trademarks and/or registered trademarks of Scholastic Inc.

The publisher does not have any control over and does not assume any
responsibility for author or third-party websites or their content.

No part of this publication may be reproduced, stored in a retrieval system, or
transmitted in any form or by any means, electronic, mechanical, photocopying,
recording, or otherwise, without written permission of the publisher.
For information regarding permission, write to Scholastic Inc.,
Attention: Permissions Department, 557 Broadway, New York, NY 10012.

This book is a work of fiction. Names, characters, places, and incidents
are either the product of the author's imagination or are used fictitiously,
and any resemblance to actual persons, living or dead, business
establishments, events, or locales is entirely coincidental.

Library of Congress Control Number: 2015951470

ISBN 978-0-545-76749-1

10 9 8 7 6 5 4 3 2 1   16 17 18 19 20

Cover, back cover, and endpapers: blueprint: © amgun/Shutterstock; map: © Map
Resources; spiral: © Herr Biter/Shutterstock; sign: © Go Bananas Design Studio/
Shutterstock; dam blueprints: Library of Congress; Cityscape: © mihaiulia/
Shutterstock; sky: © Sergey Nivens/Shutterstock and © gyn9037/Shutterstock;
hurricane diagrams: © Grolier; stormy sea: © Andrey Yurlov/Shutterstock and
© Joel Calheiros/Shutterstock. Back endpaper: Ekat crest: SJI Associates for Scholastic.
Interior images: clog page 22: © Paul Koomen/Shutterstock; mug page 42:
© microvector/Shutterstock; shield page 42: © Vector1st/Shutterstock; crown page 42:
© Ivan Ponomarev/Shutterstock; water page 58: Wojtek Starak/CG Textures; boy
"Jonah Wizard" pages 66 and 68: Ken Karp for Scholastic; bathroom pages 66 and
68 © Photographee.eu/Shutterstock; uniform page 125: Library of Congress; boy
"Hamilton" page 125: Ken Karp for Scholastic; paper page 125: CG Textures; concrete
page 158: CG Textures; fireworks page 164: © Kalenik Hanna/Shutterstock. All
other art and book and cover design created by Charice Silverman for Scholastic.

Library printing, February 2016

Printed in the U.S.A.   23

Scholastic US: 557 Broadway · New York, NY 10012
Scholastic Canada: 604 King Street West · Toronto, ON M5V 1E1
Scholastic New Zealand Limited: Private Bag 94407 · Greenmount, Manukau 2141
Scholastic UK Ltd.: Euston House · 24 Eversholt Street · London NW1 1DB

MIX
Paper from
responsible sources
FSC
www.fsc.org   FSC® C101537

CHAPTER 1

Depths of the North Sea, Undisclosed Coordinates

The dry suit, the neoprene, the diving helmet—none of it was enough to stave off the icy chill of the North Sea. Alek Spasky didn't mind the frigid water, though. It reminded him of Mother Russia and of his own bitter-cold heart.

On the other hand, the gaseous chemical elements and compounds regulated by the umbilical cable that connected his helmet to the salvage ship bobbing on the surface were really annoying. Let alone the buzz and whir in Alek's ears as the helmet valves let the gases in and then expelled his breath.

He reminded himself that the dive helmet wasn't the real problem. The real problem was the missing nuclear sub.

Cutting the darkness with his headlamp, Alek saw nothing but bubbles, sediment, and one lonely, pathetic-looking fish drifting in the shadowy water. Hundreds of feet below the surface, the sea was nearly devoid of life, and everything appeared drab and ashen in the shreds of sunlight struggling to reach the sea floor.

His lamp landed on a cluster of mineral deposits rising like knobby fingers from the sandy bottom of the sea. But the rock formation seemed to be the only distinguishable form in the desolate void surrounding him. That is, if he wasn't counting the other diver.

Alek turned his gaze on the salvage crew captain and he caught the man's attention.

The captain was wiry and weather-worn. He had a hearty laugh and a genuine smile. Alek had disliked him from the very beginning. He liked the captain even less now that he seemed unfazed by the dark expanse of nothingness stretching out before them.

They were not comrades. The captain and his crew of seamen who salvaged sunken vessels for a living, salvors for short, were hired hands. Nothing more.

As they'd ridden together out to the open sea and waves had splashed over the sides of the salvage ship, the captain had begun to reminisce about his days working as an underwater welder on oil rigs off the coast of Texas. "Those currents could rip you right off—"

"Get this straight," Alek had interrupted. "You are not to make small talk. You are not to tell stories. Your job is to deliver me to the *Kraken*, no questions asked."

Alek narrowed his eyes at the captain as they stood side by side in the depths of the barren sea. "Where is it?" Alek asked with a knife-sharp edge to his voice. "Where is the wreckage?"

After a slight pause the captain's voice crackled inside Alek's helmet. "Don't you worry. I'm sure we're just a hop, skip, and a jump away." The feed broke and then started again with another crackle. "It appears we landed slightly off course. We might have some exploring to do, but I promise we'll find your sunken vessel." At this, the captain chortled softly.

Alek detested people who had the tiresome habit of laughing when nothing was funny.

Imbeciles, the entire crew—they couldn't salvage a sunken vessel if the fate of their country depended on it. Which, in a way, it does... The thought made Alek's lips curl slightly at the corners.

The captain no doubt mistook Alek's smirk as a sign of shared lightheartedness. He gave the hand signal that meant everything was okay before turning to trudge along the sandy sea bottom.

Sure. Okay. Tread on like everything is fantastichesky, you careless excuse for a captain. I will take solace in knowing that your mixed-gas breaths are numbered. And there it finally was. With one single murderous thought, Alek at last felt calm wash over him.

The gases hissed and droned inside his helmet as he regulated his breathing once again and picked up his heavily weighted boots to follow in the captain's footsteps.

Soon after passing the oddly shaped rock formation, a dark, jagged outline emerged in the murky water a short distance away. Alek's pulse quickened. Was this it? Was this the *Kraken*?

Dozens of nuclear bombs went missing during the Cold War, but most people live blissfully unaware of all the sunken subs and crashed airplanes that disappeared along with the bombs they carried. Known as broken arrows, the lost nukes were untapped opportunities for terror and catastrophe. If only they could be recovered.

Alek's neoprene-clad skin tingled with anticipation as he took another step toward the shadowy object.

When a fire had broken out in the aft compartment of the *Kraken* decades before and it plunged to the bottom of the North Sea, Alek had been charged with covering up the calamity. As one of the Soviet Union's top KGB operatives, he'd pored over the images and sonar readings and had fabricated stories in order to maintain foreign relations.

Unable to share what he knew with anyone—Cold War secrets were well guarded—he had silently mourned the *Kraken*'s brokenness. What a waste that the sub had fallen. What a waste that the *Kraken* had never had the chance to demonstrate its awesome power.

Everything in life deserves a second chance. I deserve a second chance.

At long last Alek would emerge from the shadows.

He quickened his slog through the sea. Yet as he drew closer to the looming form, it proved not to be the sub, but instead a towering deep-sea reef. When the captain merely glanced back and shrugged before turning the corner of the closest ridge, Alek's anger flared.

As Alek rounded the corner to follow the captain, the current pushed back. It unbalanced him. It teased beneath his arms, streamed between his legs, and tugged on his helmet and boots. Tucking his head slightly, he leaned into it.

Like walking uphill in a windstorm.

Slanting forward as he went, he maneuvered around the first rocky bend only to be swept off his feet and bashed back against the reef by the flow of the sea.

The captain's voice resounded inside his helmet. "Be careful back there." *Crackle.* "The current really picks up alongside the reef. It might just pick you up and toss you around if you don't plant your boots in the sand."

Even though Alek couldn't see the captain's face, he could hear the smile in his voice. Oh, how he hated that man.

Leaning against the jagged reef for stability, Alek pulled a steel rod from a pouch on his dry suit. With the current, he couldn't spin it across his fingers the way he so enjoyed. Yet just the weight of it in his gloved hand made him feel centered again. Deadly centered.

When Alek finally worked his way around the last sharp bend, to a flat area where the current waned, the sea rewarded him by coughing up its long-forgotten treasure. Nestled behind the reef, the *Kraken* slept, covered by a blanket of barnacles and silt.

The captain stood directly in front of Alek, staring up in awe at the giant arc of the *Kraken*'s rear propeller.

Even half buried, the blades reached high above his head.

Alek ran his headlamp down the bridge of the sub and across the blanket of sludge and sediment cloaking it. There was something eerie about the wreckage and the way the sea had claimed it—rusting the steel and draping the railings with red kelp.

Over the whir and hiss of his own breathing, Alek could hear creaks and moans as the current whistled through the metal vessel. Or perhaps what he really heard were the groans and cries of a ghostly crew forever trapped inside.

Beyond the captain, the enormous missile-shaped submarine faded in the darkness. It was impossible to see from one end of the sub to the other, but Alek could tell the hull was still intact. More importantly, the nukes inside were still intact.

A broad smile cracked Alek's face.

He had everything he needed: the warheads, the cables, the equipment necessary to salvage the wreck. He also had one thing he didn't need. While the captain stood with his back to Alek, still appraising the behemoth sub, Alek raised the steel rod. He used it to slice the captain's umbilical.

CHAPTER 2

Lake Como, Italy

Trust no one. Not even Grace? The thought caused Amy Cahill's lungs to constrict. Heated pangs coursed through her body. Ever since she'd learned of her grandmother's betrayal, Amy had alternated between anguish and fury. This new wave was laced with anger.

How could she?

Amy inhaled deeply and willed the boiling emotions to settle. As she stared out the window of Jonah Wizard's European base of operations, her rage dulled.

Perhaps if she never moved again—just let her muscles atrophy and her mind weaken—she could forget Grace's dark secret. Amy focused her mind on the tranquil waters of Lake Como glistening in the moonlight. She took in the snow-capped Alps behind the smattering of Old World villas hugging the curve of the lake.

Jonah's villa stood out among the others. With its considerably large, angular frame, walls made of glass, and state-of-the-art infinity pool, it was uniquely modern. It was striking.

Grace had been one-of-a-kind, too. Brave and just . . . or so Amy had thought. Amy clenched her jaw. Apparently no view, no matter how spectacular, no amount of stillness or show of willpower could wipe away the stain that now tainted every memory Amy held of her grandmother.

Grace had been everything to Amy. Everything Amy wanted to be. But Amy had learned that Grace had ordered the assassination of her own husband, Amy's grandfather, Nathaniel Hartford. The burn started again in Amy's stomach, slower this time. A deep, smoldering ache. Her childhood was a lie.

Not only that, Amy now believed that Nathaniel was back, gunning for revenge. Grace had turned her husband into a monster, the Outcast, a man who had vowed to re-create some of history's deadliest catastrophes if Amy and her friends couldn't stop him. Grace had created a violent and vicious circle, a hurricane of evil. And Amy and her brother, Dan, were caught in the middle of it.

The noise of someone stirring downstairs broke Amy's concentration. Amy's brother and cousins had crashed the moment they'd stepped through the door of Jonah's villa. Maybe Ian was pacing again. He'd been devastated by their inability to stop the Outcast's most recent disaster. Ian Kabra was now the head of the Cahill family, and the failure weighed heaviest on him. And the Outcast wasn't through with Ian yet— wasn't through with any of them.

Amy winced. She and Dan never should've saddled Ian with the responsibility of leading the Cahills. Grace had been their grandmother, not his. She and Dan should've been the ones shouldering the fallout from her mistakes.

Even if Nathaniel isn't the Outcast, Ian isn't up to the task of leading the family. The disloyalty of the thought made her want to choke. But the truth clawed at her. *He's starting to crack.*

Another noise echoed from the lower level of the villa, but it was too high-pitched to be a person pacing this time. It sounded like the squeak of the sliding glass door.

Amy looked out the window again. Steam rose from the surface of the heated pool, creating a mist between the villa and the wishbone-shaped Lake Como. She expected to see Ian wandering outdoors, lost in his thoughts and the haze. Instead, a black-clad figure skirted through the manicured bushes hedging the pool.

"Hey! Stop!" she shouted, and pounded the glass with the palm of her hand. The figure glanced back only long enough for Amy to discern that the intruder was a woman.

The rush of adrenaline centered Amy's thoughts and deadened the ache in her stomach. It wasn't stillness that she required to distract herself from her worries. It was action. Amy spun on her heel, then barreled down the stairs.

Hamilton Holt—asleep like a boulder in the armchair—was directly in line with her path out the door. The rest of the crew—Dan, Ian, Cara, and Jonah—were lumps in the dark, spread out on all the sofas. Amy smacked Hamilton on the shoulder as she blew past. "Come on!"

"That you, Mom?" Hamilton grumbled. "Is there bacon for breakfast?"

"I'll fry enough bacon to feed a Tomas army if you catch me a burglar!" Amy yelled as she raced on, never once glancing back to see if he was moving.

The woman had left the sliding door slightly ajar. Amy tore through it and felt the crisp night air like a slap in the face.

By the time she reached the edge of the pool, Hamilton was on her heels. "Which way?" he asked without so much as a trace of grogginess left in his voice.

Amy pointed to a gap in the towering hedges. Without another word, they sprinted straight for it. Pitch-blackness engulfed them as they moved beyond the glow of the lighted pool. Amy sucked the cool air into her burning lungs. Typically, Hamilton could out-run her. But not tonight. She charged through the thicket, steps ahead of him.

When she heard the snap of a twig, Amy halted, darted to the left, and drove her arm through the brambles. Thorns clawed at the skin on her exposed wrist, but her fingers connected with something soft. She closed her fist and tugged, pulling the woman toward her by the hem of her black hooded sweatshirt. As the woman twisted and strained to pull free, the phone in Amy's pocket vibrated.

The noise and sensation divided Amy's attention for a mere fraction of a second. But it was enough for the woman to clear the bushes, swing, and strike. The blow knocked Amy back and loosened her grip on the woman's sweatshirt.

Amy felt Hamilton's arms swoop around her waist, catching her as she stumbled. Once she found her balance, she and Hamilton scanned the darkness. The woman was gone.

Amy's phone stopped ringing. Her collarbone throbbed. All she could hear was the sound of her own breathing. Then a sudden flash of light sliced the darkness, the illumination breaking through another gap in the bushes.

She and Hamilton made eye contact. "Let's go!" Amy cried. Neck and neck this time, they wove through the trees and shrubbery, then vaulted over a thick, knee-high hedge.

As soon as her feet connected with gravel, Amy picked them up again, racing for the end of the drive. When she and Hamilton reached it, a second light flashed. This time, the light went off directly in their eyes—striking them both blind.

CHAPTER 3

Mount Fuji, Japan

Nellie Gomez, Amy and Dan's legal guardian, angled the phone away from her chin. "Amy's not picking up," she told her boyfriend, Sammy Mourad. With her free hand, she slid a lock of hair away from her face, then tucked the shock of color behind her right ear.

Outside the window of the little Japanese restaurant, Mount Fuji was a nearly perfect, snow-tipped cone. The smell of *ika yakisoba*, fried noodles with squid, made Nellie's stomach growl. It sounded as delicious to her as it smelled, but they'd placed an order for grilled cheese sandwiches to go.

And go we must. Nellie only hoped her gut instinct was right. Summiting Mount Fuji this time of year was beyond risky, but that was exactly what they aimed to do.

The Cahill kids had stopped the Outcast's first disaster, but they hadn't been successful twice. The Outcast had crashed an airship, and thirty-six people had gone down with it. When images of the victims had flashed on every single media outlet, Nellie had recognized some of their faces. Many of those who'd perished had been influential leaders of the Lucian branch of the Cahill family. The first disaster had been an embarrassment for the Janus branch. It wasn't hard to connect the dots. The Outcast was targeting the four Cahill family branches, and that meant the next attack would most likely be on the Tomas or the Ekaterinas.

She needed to be at the place he didn't want them looking. If Nellie was right, that place was deep inside the heart of Mount Fuji, at the Tomas branch stronghold.

"It's about four and half degrees Celsius outside," Sammy said, interrupting her thoughts. He was gazing out the window at a round, clock-shaped thermometer with a single black hand. "That's forty degrees Fahrenheit for us—a near record high for Mount Fuji this time of year."

"Well, that at least is good news," Nellie said, clicking off her phone and slipping it back into her pack. The warmer temps didn't guarantee ideal conditions for their hike, but they did mean that she and Sammy would stand a better chance of not freezing to death. She hadn't anticipated how much of the mountain and even the area around the base would be closed.

Thankfully, this quaint café was open year-round. Now they just needed their sandwiches, so they could get on their way. As if on cue, the restaurant owner popped out of the kitchen. "Owner" might have been a little limiting in scope. The restaurateur seemed to be the owner, cook, and service staff all in one. Smiling broadly, he set down a greasy paper sack in the center of their table.

"Should have come two weeks ago," the man said. "See cherry blossoms."

Nellie returned his smile. "Thank you for the sandwiches." Even to a picky palate such as hers, warm, melted cheddar cheese and toasted white bread always tasted good. Too bad the sandwiches would be cold by the time they ate them.

"Now blossoms gone. Business slow. Won't pick up till snow melts from peak. Then hikers come back."

"That's what we're doing," Sammy said, "hiking to the summit."

Nellie kicked him beneath the table, but the damage was already done.

As Sammy bent over to rub his shin, she searched the restaurant owner's face. He didn't have an Outcast-turncoat look about him. There were laugh lines around his mouth and kindness in the wrinkled folds encircling his dark eyes. There was also concern and what Nellie perceived as fear for her and Sammy's well-being.

Maybe Sammy's slipup hadn't done any harm after all.

As the man gave a polite bow and backed away from the table, Nellie heard him whisper under his breath, "Avalanche season." Then, even quieter, *Cho beriba.*

"Avalanches? *Cho beriba?*" Sammy asked as soon as the old man was out of earshot.

Nellie was well versed in several foreign languages, although her Japanese was rusty. "The avalanche risk *is* high right now . . . and *cho beriba* is slang. It means 'very bad,' I think. No. Not 'very bad' . . . 'extraordinarily bad.' I'm pretty sure he thinks climbing Mount Fuji is a rotten idea. At least it is this time of year."

Sammy whipped out his own phone and began researching the treacherous trek ahead of them. "The resting huts and facilities on the way to the top are all still closed for the winter," he reported gravely.

"Uh-huh."

"You knew that already?"

Nellie shrugged. "Maybe . . . but you know as well as I do that we don't have the luxury of waiting around until the snow melts and the resting huts open. We have to find out what the Outcast is up to. Today."

"How do the Tomas do it?" Sammy wondered aloud.

"You forget that the Tomas are all adrenaline junkies," Nellie said. "They live for testing their endurance."

When she noticed the anxiety rising on her boyfriend's gorgeous face, she added, "Don't worry. We've got the right gear. Plus, we'll stop at Fujiyoshida Sengen Shrine to say a prayer before ascending."

"Yeah, that'll keep us safe for sure." Sammy cracked a lopsided smile.

Nellie clutched his hand and gave it a reassuring squeeze. "Can't hurt, right?"

They stood from the table and exited the restaurant with their fingers still woven together. But when they stepped outside, Nellie saw something that changed her mind about the shrine. A stop was definitely off the docket: The mercury in the thermometer hadn't dropped the hand a single notch. The air was balmy and the sun was still shining, but the dark clouds on the horizon were more than a little unsettling.

They'd need every last minute of fair weather to scale the mountain.

CHAPTER 4

Lake Como, Italy

There was a reason her friend had been nicknamed the Hammer. Before Amy had a chance to let him know that the man holding the camera wasn't the intruder, Hamilton wound his arm back and let it fly.

The man doubled over in pain.

"Wait, Ham!" Amy said, stopping her brawny friend from landing a second punch. "The intruder was a woman."

"Oh, dude. I'm sorry," Ham said, reaching out to the man. "Can I hold your camera for you? While you, uh, recover?" Something about the grin on his face told Amy that Hamilton had known all along that the man wasn't their burglar.

The stranger recoiled, still bent over, and clutched the camera to his chest. "Get away from me!" he groaned. The man was obviously American—white T-shirt, Oakland Raiders hat worn backward, holey blue jeans. He stuck out in Lake Como even more than Jonah's villa did.

"Who are you?" Amy asked, narrowing her eyes at the stranger. Then the pieces clicked into place. Her cousin Jonah Wizard was a teenage superstar, and the man was here to take photos and sell them to the media. Hamilton was Jonah's bodyguard. He'd dealt with paparazzi many times. No wonder he didn't look remorseful for having knocked the wind out of this guy.

The man didn't answer Amy's question. But he didn't have to. The way he and Hamilton were staring each other down basically confirmed it.

"There were two flashes. Did you take a photo of anyone else?" Amy asked. "There was a woman who came this way . . ." she added, trying to prod the man along.

The man glared on.

"I'll take that as a yes," Ham said.

The paparazzo straightened his back, then spit on the gravel near their feet. "Who are you two?" He glanced back and forth between Amy and Hamilton and the striking glass-walled villa at the end of the drive. A light seemed to reenter the man's eyes and he set his jaw and jutted his chin. "Wait a minute. I know you." He stared right at Amy. "You're one of those rich Cahill kids, am I right?"

No. Not a light. A money-hungry gleam.

Amy fought the urge to wallop the man herself. Disgusted, she spun toward Ham. "Look. You get the camera. I'll go wake the others."

Hamilton nodded. He grinned menacingly at the paparazzo.

The man whimpered and clutched his camera tighter.

"Oh, and try not to hit him again," Amy said. *"Too hard."*

Dan Cahill stirred when Amy flicked on the lights. "Why aren't you sleeping?" he asked blearily. His sister was moving too quickly and talking too fast for him to keep up.

Before he'd fizzled out, the shocking news about Grace had been swimming around in his head like a barracuda doing laps in a swimming pool. A little sleep should've helped. But now that he was awake, he was more confused than ever.

Amy was saying something about a burglar and a Popsicle, or maybe he'd been dreaming about a Popsicle, but Amy had definitely said something that started with a P. "Did you say a burglar stole a Popsicle?" Dan mumbled. That seemed ridiculous, even to his sluggish brain.

Dan almost closed his eyes and went back to sleep, hoping things would seem less garbled in the morning. But the grave expression on Amy's face told him that this was serious. Not just a cruel prank, waking him up after not nearly enough Zs. Besides, a cruel prank was something he would pull. Not Amy.

His head hurt from lack of sleep, but Dan slowly drew himself to an upright position on the couch. The world had seemed a little upside down since he'd found out about Grace. Now it was virtually spinning. He blinked his eyes rapidly. As his surroundings finally came into focus, he noticed that someone was missing. "Where's Ham?" he asked.

"Outside. Dealing with our rodent problem," Amy said. Then she gently shook Ian and Cara awake on opposite ends of the sofa. Too tired to get up, Dan tossed a pillow at Jonah where he lay drooling on the rug.

"A burglar, a Popsicle, *and* a rodent problem?" Dan wondered aloud.

"What?" Amy questioned. "I never said anything about a Popsicle. I said the *paparazzo*."

Amy repeated the entire story for everyone to hear. It made much more sense now that Dan was fully awake. "Let's figure out what the woman took," he said, glancing around. The room certainly didn't appear to have been ransacked.

Jonah's decor took minimalism to an extreme, but there were still a few expensive vases and brightly colored art on the wall. There wasn't much in the way of things to be looted. And, scarce as they were, all the pricey pieces appeared to have been untouched.

"Check your personal belongings," Amy directed the group. "The Outcast might be trying to lift information off one of us. He could've sent someone to steal our devices."

Ian scoffed at the idea. "He humiliated me in front of all the branch leaders. He had me forcefully escorted out of my own home. He's taken my family and my pride. What more could he possibly want?"

"This isn't all about you, Ian. Remember?" said Dan. "Four disasters. There have only been two. Maybe this has something to do with the third."

"Or maybe the whole thing is entirely unrelated," Cara Pierce offered. "I've checked my stuff. Laptop, cell phone, wallet—it's all here. Maybe Jonah has a stalker." She turned to face the teenage superstar. "Doesn't that happen to you all the time? Maybe the intruder wanted a memento. Maybe she took something that you wouldn't expect anyone to want. Maybe she took something creepy."

"Yeah, like your toothbrush," Dan said, "or a lock of hair."

Jonah's hand shot to his buzz cut and he fingered it for bald patches as Dan continued surveying the room. An unusual object sitting on the glass coffee table caught his eye. "Or maybe she didn't take anything at all. Maybe the intruder *left* something. That's not really your style, is it, Jonah?"

Dan pointed and everyone's eyes followed. Jonah seemed thankful for both the diversion and the fact that his hair was still intact. Jonah scooped the item up. It was a wooden shoe, and the clog was intricately painted. It showed a pretty scene with a windmill overlooking a canal. The canal was lined with colorful tulips that extended down and graced the rounded toe with a splash of red.

From where Dan was seated, he could make out words painted on the bottom, but not what they said. "Flip it over, Wiz," he muttered, his words heavy with foreboding. It would've been nice if things had calmed down for at least a few days. Instead, not only was the storm not letting up, it was *picking* up. A sense of dread pierced Dan's gut as Jonah read aloud:

> "'Disaster Three. Water marches on land.
> Inaction leads to more blood on your hands.
> Arrows are broken, lessons unlearned.
> Inert responses, power unearned.
> Katrina wreaked profound devastation,

The same fate awaits a new coastal nation. . . .
The Gateway floods when autonomy fails,
The torrent erases the Dutch king's trail.
A violent surge, a breach in the wall,
The House of Orange will crumble and fall.'"

While everyone else sat there, stunned into silence, Dan moaned. "The Outcast is going to attack Holland." He'd always been fast at piecing things together. The wooden shoe, the windmills, the Dutch king, the coastal nation—it was obvious where the next disaster was going to take place. And Katrina? The storm wasn't just picking up. It was going to reach fever pitch.

There definitely wouldn't be any rest. They had to plan for the largest catastrophe yet—devastation to rival Hurricane Katrina.

CHAPTER 5

Lake Como, Italy

Ian Kabra wanted blood. *And what a Kabra wants, a Kabra gets*, he thought.

"Forget Holland," he commanded. If there was anything a Lucian knew, anything a Kabra knew, it was how to cut to the chase. "We know where the Outcast is: at our home in Attleboro. We know the house better than anyone. We *built* the defenses. It's time to go nuclear." He paused, making sure all eyes were on him. "I say we orchestrate our own disaster and rain it down on the Outcast's head. We'll need poison, a team of assassins, and—"

Amy and Cara exchanged a look. "What?" he snapped.

Cara cleared her throat. She did that adorable thing where she rolled her lips inward and smiled while her face pinched with concern. "It's just that you seem a little . . . unhinged."

Ian's eyes narrowed. "You don't know what you're saying. My response is entirely justifiable, and retaliation is *clearly* in order. Those were Lucian leaders who died when the airship exploded, may I remind you. Some of their children were friends of mine. Take Duncan Wittenberg, for example. He and I played cricket together in primary school. Now both of his parents are gone." Ian threw out his arms. "I can't just let that go."

"Nobody is denying that what happened is terrible, or saying that you shouldn't be upset. We're just worried about you," Cara said. "We don't want you to crack. The airship was a hard blow, but—"

"We don't *kill* people. We *save* people," Amy jumped in. "That's the difference between the good guys and the bad guys." She paused like she was thinking of something or someone else, before adding, "We don't want to sink to the Outcast's level."

Heat burned Ian's cheeks. It was bad enough to have Cara needling him, but to be double-teamed was utterly unacceptable. He needed a retort. It shouldn't be hard, considering his outstanding intellectual acumen. But before he could find the proper words to put them both back in their places, Hamilton burst in through the sliding glass door. "What'd I miss?" he said.

"Well done!" Amy said, then snatched an expensive-looking camera from his hands. "Now we can see who the Outcast sent to do his dirty work." She whirled around and held the camera out to Cara. "Will you do us the honor?"

Cara nodded. With the speed and fluidity of a natural born hacker, she whipped out her laptop, flipped it open, and reached for the camera.

While she was busy clicking through a number of images on her screen, Hamilton sidled up next to Ian. "Everything okay? You seem a little . . . unhinged," Ham said.

Ian turned his scowl on Ham, crossed his arms over his chest, and smoldered. *Why does everyone have to keep saying that?*

"How'd you get the camera, Ham?" Amy asked. "You didn't . . ." her voice trailed off.

"He's not on his way to the hospital or anything, if that's what you mean," Hamilton replied. "It just took a little bargaining, but we finally settled on a price."

"You paid that scumbag?"

"Not with money." Hamilton's eyes shifted to where Jonah was sitting nearby on the leather couch.

"Yo, why are you looking at me like that?" Jonah had been giving the wooden shoe a closer examination. He set it back down on the glass coffee table.

"You remember a few weeks back when I caught you reciting Shakespeare?" Ham stifled a laugh. "And you were, like, practicing your duckface in the mirror between lines."

"Yes," Jonah said through clenched teeth.

"Remember how I caught some of it on video with my phone? Well, the paparazzo seemed really interested in the clip. I thought it was a decent trade." Hamilton's mouth stretched into a grin.

Jonah picked up the wooden shoe again, gripped it like a weapon, and charged.

"Guys, I hate to interrupt," Cara said, "but I have something here."

Skidding to a halt, Jonah let the shoe fall to his side as everyone gathered around Cara's laptop. They stared at the image on the screen of a stunning woman with dark skin and dreads peeking out from under her hood. Her deep brown eyes had been wide with surprise when the paparazzo snapped the photo. Ian's heart sank. Even with the hood, he recognized her immediately.

So did Jonah. "Mom?" he croaked. Jonah's face went carefully blank, as if he had retreated to someplace deep inside. Ian looked away. Contrary to what Cara and Amy thought, Ian was quite capable of empathy. He knew how it felt to have your own mother betray you. He knew how it felt to swallow so much hurt and humiliation that you thought you might drown.

Ian sank a little in his expensive loafers and concentrated on all the fine qualities he possessed. He was talented, charming, intelligent, and strong-willed, along with the added bonus of being dashingly good looking. He was born and raised to lead. Obviously.

So why am I starting to hate it?

The answer was, in part, because of moments like this one. Ian wasn't done ranting. There was nothing he wanted more than to continue his outburst. Even if a deadly assault wasn't the proper play, he still had plenty of rage to purge. But his friend was hurting, and as leader, it fell on Ian to turn the tide.

Ian walked over to Jonah and awkwardly placed a hand on his friend's shoulder. "I know this is rather unsettling for you, Jonah. For all of us, really, but we need to focus. The Outcast has sent us a message. What do we know?"

"Well," Cara said, glancing up from her computer, "for one thing, this disaster has the potential to be even deadlier than the *Hindenburg* and *Titanic* reenactments combined. Hurricane Katrina caused more than 1,800 deaths and was the most costly catastrophe in American history. When the levees failed following the storm, there were places in New Orleans submerged under as much as twenty feet of water. More than one hundred billion gallons flooded the streets, and hundreds of thousands of people were displaced from their homes. The scale of this disaster . . . it's massive. It's something much larger than the Outcast's first two reenactments." Cara's eyes were huge as she looked up at him. "I just don't see how we're going to be able to contain something like this."

Quiet overtook the room and all eyes fell on Ian. For a fleeting moment, he missed the old days, when expectations dropped like lead on Amy and Dan instead. He smoothed the wrinkles in his slacks, and for the first time, noticed that a shirttail was hanging out. He swiftly tucked it back in. "Okay. Then we need to track any storms brewing in the vicinity of Holland."

"I'm already a step ahead of you," Cara said. In a gesture that was vexingly cute, she shot him a crooked smile before she continued. "It's officially called the Netherlands, by the way, and the weather patterns look clear for the next ten days."

"Perhaps we have the location wrong, then. Perhaps it's not the Netherlands that the Outcast is targeting," Ian responded. "Have you looked for tropical storm warnings anywhere else in the world? Is there a typhoon headed for Japan, perhaps, or a hurricane in the Caribbean?"

Cara shook her head. "I don't think so. The Outcast has been overt this time. He mentioned the Dutch king and that 'The House of Orange will crumble and fall.' The House of Orange is another name for the royal family of the Netherlands. We should focus our attention there."

Hamilton let out a sigh of relief. "Then we can all just go back to sleep, right? No big storms for the next ten days. We have some time to recover. I, for one, am looking forward to swimming laps in Jonah's pool tomorrow. A little stress relief, a little planning, and then we hit the Netherlands."

"I don't think that's such a hot idea either," Cara said. "The rest of the riddle—inaction, arrows that are broken, inert responses, lessons unlearned—it's seething with double meaning. Much of the devastation caused by Hurricane Katrina wasn't blamed on the storm itself. Experts called it a systemic failure." She caught Ian's eye. "Those who were charged with preventing this type of catastrophe let down the people of New Orleans. And so did all the emergency responders after the levees failed."

Ian reddened. What was she implying?

" 'Power unearned,' " Dan chimed in. "He's saying we don't deserve to lead the Cahills. And, arrows, those totally have a symbolic meaning of defense. The Outcast is saying that we're broken. We failed to defend the airship, and if we don't stay on our toes, this levee failure in the Netherlands—it's going to be on our hands, too."

Ian couldn't stop himself from glancing down at his own hands. He was in desperate need of a manicure, but worse, they felt ineffectual. After failing to stop the second disaster, he'd felt *ineffectual*. It wasn't a sensation he was accustomed to. And he didn't like it any more than he liked dealing with other people's problems.

Perhaps he'd been a little hasty in his long-held belief that he'd surpassed his role model, Napoleon Bonaparte—a fine Lucian strategist if ever there was one. Ian hated to admit it, but with the fresh taste of defeat in his mouth, he thought he might actually have sunk to Napoleon's level.

Even though Napoleon had succeeded in conquering the world, he'd ultimately suffered defeat at that distasteful affair, the Battle of Waterloo. Although that wasn't the first time Napoleon had been forced to abdicate his throne and be sent into exile. The allies had invaded France in 1814 and sent Napoleon to exile on the island of Elba. But he'd escaped and immediately reclaimed his empire.

The cheerful thought struck Ian that the airship disaster was merely his island of Elba. It wasn't too late to outshine Napoleon. When history books were written about Ian Kabra, there would be no Battle of Waterloo.

Ian puffed out his chest, but no one around him seemed to notice. They were all gripped by whatever it was Dan had been saying.

"Look, I know I was, like, just a little dweeb when Hurricane Katrina went down," Dan continued, "but sometimes my memory is a colossal curse.

"I can still see the images that ran on the news. Cars floating down the street and people stuck on rooftops. And rooftops were, like, the only thing you could see. Houses, buildings, gas stations—everything was completely submerged in water."

Hamilton groaned as he gazed out the window at the pool. "Maybe I don't feel much like going for a swim after all."

"It's settled, then," Ian said in a voice as commanding as his war-hungry Lucian predecessor. "It is time to prepare for battle, chaps, and we will be victorious! There will be no Waterloo!"

To that, Ian was met with nothing but blank stares. He cleared his throat and tried again. "Er, storm or no storm, we leave for the Netherlands first thing in the morning."

CHAPTER 6

Attleboro, Massachusetts

The Outcast set up troops outside the village. He speculated that a team of archers, goblins, and barbarians would do the trick. The number was great enough to launch a strong attack but would leave him enough manpower for his true objective.

The strategy video game on his tablet was mildly entertaining. He preferred a real-life chessboard and a living opponent sitting across from him. That was, as long as the opponent was worthy. His butler, Mr. Berman, was not.

As the Outcast's online adversaries reacted to the attack, he took note of the time. The children would've received his latest work of poetry by now. The wheels were in motion. Whether the children lived or died made no difference to him. That was what set him apart. That was why he won when others lost.

Family was valuable only as long as it made you strong. If loyalty was blind or attachments ran too deep, family could be a great weakness. Family had been Grace's undoing.

There'd never been any doubt that Grace was ruthless. But she never seemed to understand that if you truly wanted to win, sacrifices had to be made—even painful sacrifices.

While the online villagers were distracted by his troops, the Outcast would make his real move. He couldn't care less about his dying archers, barbarians, and goblins. He'd make no rescue attempts. Hiding behind the chaos he'd created, he'd secretly search for the dark elixir—the elixir that would eradicate his enemies forever.

Perhaps this game did possess some improvements over chess, after all.

"Excuse me," Mr. Berman interrupted.

Mr. Berman had a biddable nature. He'd been an easy play when the Outcast needed to slide someone into position at Grace's estate before the takeover. The Outcast's only regret was that he hadn't purchased the loyalty of someone with a quicker wit and a better poker face. The butler bored him.

The Outcast set down his tablet. "What is it?"

"I just thought you should be made aware that Nellie Gomez and Sammy Mourad were spotted departing a plane at Mount Fuji Shizuoka Airport. That's the closest airport to the Tomas stronghold. Should we alert Magnus?"

The Outcast pressed his fingertips together and breathed deeply. "No."

"No?"

"Do you need me to repeat myself?" The Outcast sharpened his tone. If Magnus knew he was at risk of being detected, he might abort his assignment. The Tomas leader was but one cog in the wheel, and the Outcast needed him to keep turning in order for the project to reach completion. "If Nellie and Sammy somehow manage to make it inside the stronghold, I'm certain Magnus is more than capable of dealing with them."

"Very well, sir."

As Mr. Berman turned to leave the room, Amy and Dan's Egyptian Mau sprang from out of nowhere and landed with all four paws on the Outcast's tablet. Saladin arched his back and hissed in the Outcast's face.

The Outcast snatched Saladin up by the scruff of his neck, but the damage had already been done. One of Saladin's paws had landed on a button, releasing healing potion to all the Outcast's troops. He no longer had enough energy to go searching for the elixir.

"Mr. Berman!" the Outcast yelled as Saladin hissed again and cleaved the air, trying to claw the Outcast's unnaturally taut face. "Dispose of this cat!"

Ruthlessness applied to family pets, as well.

Mountain Fuji, Japan

The conditions on Mount Fuji were far worse than they'd appeared from below.

Teeth chattering as he spoke, Sammy said, "Maybe we sh-should've st-stopped by the Yosha . . . Yoshi . . ."

"The Fujiyoshida Sengen Shrine?" Nellie supplied.

Sammy nodded.

They hadn't stopped to say a prayer to Princess Konohanasakuya, the Shinto deity associated with Mount Fuji, because of the clouds rolling in. Passing through the wooden torii gates of the traditional shrine on the north side of the mountain and starting the climb at the Yoshida trailhead would have added five hours to their trek.

But if they *had* stopped at the shrine, perhaps Princess Konohanasakuya would've blown the clouds a different direction.

Instead, they'd done what most climbers did these days, and started halfway up the Yoshida Trail. The Fuji Subaru Line, the windy road leading to the Fifth Station, had just opened up and they were able to bypass the beginning of the trail by hopping on a shuttle.

Of course, when the majority of climbers chose the shorter route and skipped the shrine at the bottom of the mountain, it was late summer. The princess was probably in a better mood in the mild months of July and August than she was during the tumultuous month of April.

Even with the balaclava that covered most of her face, Nellie had to tuck her head beneath her arm with each new violent gust of wind. And the record high temp that Sammy had noted—a balmy forty degrees—was only working against them.

The snow was soft instead of icy. The spikes she and Sammy had strapped to their boots were sinking into the sludge instead of gaining traction. They'd been at it for nearly two hours when a long, dull rumble—as if the mountain were a sleeping giant, groaning and moaning awake—reached her ears. Nellie jolted and her gloved hands trembled.

When the grumbling stopped, she swallowed her fear and lifted one spiked boot from the wet, heavy snow. It sank knee-deep again as she slowly inched forward. She glanced back to see how Sammy was faring. When she did, she found that he'd fallen behind as he, too, fought for every step.

Sammy looked every bit as frightened and tired as she felt, but there wasn't a good place to stop. There'd be no shelter from the elements until they reached the stronghold. Japan's highest peak was swathed in snow but almost entirely barren of trees. The path stretching to the skyline was a solid blanket of white.

Through the slits of his mask, Sammy petitioned with his eyes. He wanted to turn around, but there was no way Nellie was caving. The Outcast was up to something and she needed to know what. They had to reach the summit.

"Come on!" she yelled. "Pick up those feet!" She didn't want to be harsh with Sammy, but if she went easy on him, he'd never make it.

Sammy gritted his teeth and glared back at her.

That's right, Nellie thought. *Get angry*. "Move it! Move it! Move it!" she chanted as he slogged forward. When

Sammy finally caught up, Nellie's face broke into a tentative smile. "I knew you could do it."

Nellie bit her lip, worried she'd pushed him too hard.

But after Sammy stopped gasping and caught his breath, he laughed into his balaclava. "I didn't realize the point of this exercise was to go all Hamilton Holt on me. What's next on the agenda: circuit training or a toning class?"

The vise around Nellie's heart released. "Maybe I'll make you do both," she countered. "You better watch out, science geek. When we reach the top, the Tomas will have plenty of equipment to whip you into shape. First things first, though. Let's finish scaling this mountain. I can feel the temperature dropping as we speak."

"Speaking as a science geek, if the temps drop enough, the snow will harden and it'll be easier to walk," Sammy said.

Just then, a blast of cold whisked up a small snow devil. It whirled around like a mini tornado between them. "Think what you want, geek boy," Nellie said, "but I prefer this slush to whatever the gusts are blowing in."

Sammy cast a worried look at the darkening sky. "You might be right." With that, he yanked his boot out of the snow and lurched forward.

As Nellie started off after him, she saw something that froze her to the core. An invisible knife seemed to be carving a jagged line through the white canvas of snow thirty feet above them. An earsplitting *crack* rang through the air, and Nellie's heart seized in her chest. What should've been a heartbeat later, the fissure opened wide and a slab of white separated from the mountainside.

"Sammy!" she screamed as a swell of powder rippled and barreled toward her. His head swiveled on his shoulders. But if he answered her cry, she couldn't hear him through the booming rumble that came along with the rapidly descending snow.

Gaining speed and substance as it went, the avalanche kicked up a billowing white cloud. The cloud blotted the sky. The sliding snow moved like a crashing wave coming straight for her. It was erasing everything in its path.

Nellie tried to launch herself up and to the side, aiming for the higher terrain where Sammy stood. The last clear vision she had before the ground rolled from beneath her was his outstretched hand and terror flooding his eyes. It matched the terror cleaving her chest.

Picked up by the torrent and pitched like a rag doll down the slope, she lost all awareness of which way was up and which way down. She rolled. She tumbled. The endless white engulfed her. Nellie was only able to measure the world by each new blow it dealt her.

She was lifted time and again, only to then be cast against the hard earth. Had she been carried ten feet? A hundred? She didn't know. All the while, a barrage

of rock—also snared by the cascading snow—battered her sides. Her face. Her legs. There wasn't a square inch of her body left unbruised.

Nellie searched for something to stop her fall. But with a nearly treeless slope, Mount Fuji offered nothing to anchor herself to as the tide surged. So instead, she thrashed her arms and kicked her legs. In a mock swim, she tried her best to stay afloat and not sink too deep beneath the layers.

When it finally stopped, Nellie was lying on her back; at least she thought she was. She was buried and unable to tell for certain. The only thing truly discernible about her surroundings was that she was trapped in a tiny space with very little air. That's when panic really set in.

Her stomach muscles constricted. Her rib cage felt like prison bars around her thudding heart. Her lungs gulped air greedily. She was trapped, buried alive.

Nellie knew she had to get her breathing under control. Hyperventilate, and she'd suffocate that much sooner. She forced her lungs to slow down, but she couldn't stop the shivering. Icy trembles of fear coursed through her body. Enveloped by snow, the chances were slim that Sammy would find her before it was too late.

A tear slipped from Nellie's eye. It moistened her cheek. But instead of trickling down to her chin, the tear ran to her right ear.

Gravity, Nellie thought. *I'm not on my back. I'm on my side.*

She twisted and shoved her left hand through the snow, determinedly plowing a path opposite the direction the tear had fallen. When her fist met what felt like concrete, she didn't stop. She punched through it, and just like that, her hand was free.

Nellie wasn't buried as deep as she'd originally thought. Her "swimming" had worked. Her heart thrummed with hope as her fingers wriggled in the open air. When someone grasped the hand that had broken through the snow a few minutes late, it nearly burst with relief.

Sammy dug her out and clutched her to his chest. Nellie threw her arms around his neck and rested her chin on his left shoulder. She was sore but nothing was broken. She'd been battered, but she was still alive.

By the way Sammy was trembling beneath her grasp she could tell that he'd been equally traumatized. She had to let him know that she was all right. That everything would be okay.

Over the whipping winds, she spoke in as light a tone as she could muster. "Should we say that prayer to Princess Konohanasakuya now?"

CHAPTER 7

Lake Como, Italy

"Are we making a mistake?" Dan whispered.

"What do you mean?" Amy whispered back. Her eyes flicked toward the kitchen, where Ian sat, sipping English breakfast tea from a coffee mug that read *The WIZ is king.*

"Do we need to try harder to find out who the Outcast really is?" Dan bunched his lips together, gathering his thoughts before he went on. "Listen. He got to Ian's dad and Jonah's mom, and he killed Aunt Beatrice. He's obviously got some serious ties to the family. If we can figure out his true identity, it'll help us figure out his endgame. Then we can start being protractive instead of reactive."

"Proactive," Amy amended.

Dan looked for the twinkle he typically found gleaming in his sister's eye when she corrected him. It wasn't there, and that worried him. There'd been a tighter pinch to Amy's face ever since they'd found out about Grace.

When he'd learned the news, he'd felt like he'd been inside a snow globe that someone picked up and rattled around. But things were starting to settle. Amy and Grace had been much closer. He suspected Amy's globe had been smashed and he didn't know how to help her glue the pieces back together.

Dan wanted to say something to comfort his sister, but he wasn't good at that stuff. So instead he said, "Er, yeah, you know what I mean—we need to get a step ahead of him."

"Okay." Amy nodded in agreement, still solemn. "Do you have any suggestions?"

He'd been puzzling this over in his head all morning. "At first I thought Aunt Beatrice's murder was a threat, but what if she was killed because she had to be silenced?" Dan dragged a forefinger across his throat to get a laugh.

"Don't be so macabre," Amy said. She looked away and Dan wanted to kick himself. *Bad joke, worse timing.*

"Sorry. My point is that our aunt knew more about Grace and Nathaniel than anyone. She would have known them when they first got married. So if Nathaniel *is* the Outcast . . . Know what I'm sayin'?"

That caught Amy's attention. "You're saying maybe Aunt Beatrice knew something the Outcast wants to keep hidden. Maybe the key to stopping the Outcast lies in the past."

"Exactly. Aunt Beatrice's will is going to be read tomorrow at her house in Boston. Maybe there's something we could learn. Aunt Beatrice always found a way to get in the last word. I don't think she'd let a little thing like death stop her now."

That got a smile from Amy. "Are you thinking what I'm thinking?"

"That some of us need to go to the Netherlands and some of us have to be at that reading?" Dan replied. "Yeah."

"We'll have two separate teams, then." Ian broke in on their conversation. "A two-pronged attack." His voice was steady today, if a bit cool, and Dan spun around to face him. Somehow Ian had found the time for a wardrobe change and was wearing freshly pressed slacks and an expensive yet sporty polo. Dan was wearing the wrinkled clothes he'd crashed in the night before.

Dan hadn't realized that Ian was listening in. And, strangely, Dan felt a wave of guilt, which made him angry. He and Amy had just been talking. It wasn't like they were strategizing a takeover behind Ian's back.

"Cara, Dan, and I will book the next available flight to the Netherlands," Ian continued. "Amy, you and Hamilton will go with Jonah and take his Gulfstream back to Boston."

Amy's breath hitched and a splotch of red blossomed on her throat. Dan knew what she was thinking.

The Outcast was raising the stakes. He was planning a disaster that could kill thousands.

The thought of being separated from Amy at a time like this panicked Dan, too. The Cahill kids were cousins, and a team, but Amy and Dan were brother and sister. It was always the two of them and they always had each other's backs, and yet . . . Amy released the breath she'd been holding. Dan could see her eyes soften. "Okay by you, Dan?" She held his gaze. "You in the Netherlands, me in Boston?"

A rush of pride filled Dan's chest. "Yeah," he said. "Neither of us are helpless kids anymore."

The smile Amy gave him was bittersweet. She held his gaze a while longer before turning to Ian. "Sounds like a plan," she said.

Just then, Cara entered from the next room. She laced her arm through Ian's with her hand coming to rest upon his waist. "So, we're off to Amsterdam?"

Ian tensed, but didn't move away from Cara's embrace. He gave a curt nod.

For his part, Dan couldn't keep track of when the two were swooning over each other and when they hated each other's guts. But the crack in Ian's pretentious facade that they'd all seen after the airship went down seemed overall to have drawn Cara closer to him. Like his vulnerability was in some way appealing.

The whole thing made Dan want to puke.

"Great," he whispered in his sister's ear. "My team has a date with disaster and I'm the third wheel."

CHAPTER 8

Mount Fuji, Japan

Temperatures had dipped well below freezing, the peak was wrapped in heavy clouds, and the icy wind was unrelenting. But at least the path remained more or less solid for the rest of Nellie and Sammy's trek to the summit.

All Sammy wanted to do when he reached the top of Mount Fuji was stay collapsed in the snow forever. But Nellie had other plans. "Please," she said. "I know you're tired, but we can't rest just yet. Help me move this boulder aside. I don't like the look of those clouds, and we didn't survive an avalanche just to get stuck in a blizzard."

Sammy widened his eyes at her. "I think you're greatly overestimating my ability to heave aside heavy objects. I spent all my time at Columbia in the labs. I don't even know if there was a gym on campus."

"More lifting, less talking."

He let her help him back to his feet. Then he sized up the boulder. "Are you sure this is the way in? This seems like an odd entrance for the stronghold of a wealthy and influential branch. I mean, what do the Tomas have against doors?"

"Nothing," Nellie said. "But we're not going in through the front door. We're sneaking in the back."

Sammy assessed the boulder once more. It was as tall as he was and twice as wide. He understood quantum physics. He could solve complex math calculations in his head. He could not roll aside a giant rock the way Hercules, or a Tomas, could. But he'd seen enough of the brawny branch members to know that showing up unannounced at their front door didn't constitute a great idea, either.

Squatting down, he got a decent grip on the rock and threw his back into it. At the same time, Nellie pushed from the side.

He huffed and heaved for what seemed like forever, then collapsed to his knees. "It didn't budge an inch," he said, wheezing with exhaustion. It took all he had to shout over the winds whipping around them, "We're never getting in this way!"

"Uh-uh, I don't like you just for that pretty face of yours," Nellie yelled over the snow. The storm was really picking up. Flakes clumped together on her eyelashes as she spoke. "You can figure out a way to get past this boulder. Just put that brilliant mind of yours to good use."

Sammy grinned. "Show me what you brought, then, but I can't make any promises."

Nellie slid a pack off her shoulders. She'd lugged all the "worst-case-scenario" stuff up the mountain.

Sammy's own pack was jammed full of electronic devices and a "secret weapon" to bypass the security measures once they were inside the stronghold.

Digging through the pack Nellie handed him, he pulled out a handful of carabiners and a few ropes. He measured the weight of them in his hands. "These might just work," he said.

Nellie charged him with a hug, and Sammy's face flushed behind his balaclava. "*Might. I said might*," he reminded her as they pulled apart.

Sammy was rapt with determination as he set about weaving the ropes through the carabiners and creating a complex system of pulleys. Fifteen minutes later, his fingers were frozen, but the boulder was all rigged up. "Ready?" he asked Nellie.

She nodded and gripped a rope between her gloved hands.

"Go!" Sammy tugged hard. Nellie tugged harder.

The boulder jerked, then slowly rolled aside. Nellie whooped with joy as the tunnel to the Tomas stronghold opened up before them.

"For some reason I didn't expect the Tomas to have portraits hanging in their hallways," Sammy said. He listed the names of the famous people depicted in the paintings as he meandered forward. "Ulysses S. Grant. George Washington. Annie Oakley. Neil Armstrong. Seriously? Isn't hanging art more of a Janus thing? Where are the skis, the surfboards, the trophies, the gold medals, the—"

"Lower your voice," Nellie whispered. "We may not know exactly what we're looking for, but we don't want anyone to know we're here while we figure that out. Got it?"

The passageway behind the boulder had been a narrow tunnel carved through rock. No one could've caught them in it unaware. Now that they'd passed through a vent and were walking down an open hallway, they were much more vulnerable to detection. Sammy nodded, embarrassed that he'd lost his head for a moment. He blamed it on the altitude.

"Good. The scanner should be just up ahead," Nellie said.

Sammy reached over his left shoulder, grabbed hold of his pack, and then pulled it forward. The hallway was more or less a reception area. They'd sneaked in, but they weren't truly inside the stronghold yet. Sammy wasn't worried, though. Bypassing the fingerprint scanner would be a cinch.

Earlier that morning, he'd hacked into the Tomas files and pulled fingerprints of a high-ranking leader. Then he'd whipped up a batch of ballistic gelatin.

"This stuff is so cool," he told Nellie. "It's a little like Jell-O, and awesome for simulating human tissue. I just imprinted the fingerprint onto the gel and, voilà—synthetic thumb!" Having gently tugged it from his pack while he'd been talking, he now proudly held it out for her to admire.

"Best secret weapon ever," Nellie said.

He smiled and carried the thumb gingerly cupped in his hands. He was still admiring his handiwork as he approached the scanner.

"Um, Sammy? You can put that away," Nellie said.

Sammy at last glanced up. "What? Nooo!"

"Sorry." Nellie shrugged. "Don't you hear the sirens? Keep it out if you want, but the door is already open."

Sure enough, the bank vault–like hatch was swung all the way open on its hinge. Even weirder were the flashing lights and the humming sound of sirens coming from inside. He'd been too busy geeking out over his ballistic gel to notice.

Nellie and Sammy shared a look, then stepped through the doorway together. The space around them opened up a hundredfold. Sammy had never seen anything like it. The magnitude of the inside arena was insane. Every type of court, field, and sports track imaginable spread out beneath them as they stood on a steel balcony overlooking the enormous space.

Other than a row of plush box seats affixed at the same level as the steel balcony, the walls of the stronghold were bare natural rock. Everything else was super-high tech. The Tomas had made good use of the inside of their mountain, and had spared no expense when it came to outfitting their headquarters with all the latest and greatest sports equipment.

A glass-domed roof provided natural lighting for the arena, and an indoor ski slope made up one entire side of the stronghold. On the opposite side, a giant LED screen was rolling footage of athletic challenges from around the globe. But there was no one, save Nellie and himself, around to watch it.

A chill ran up Sammy's spine. Here was this amazing space, but it was utterly vacant.

A gondola was running up the indoor snow hill, but there weren't any snowboarders or skiers getting off at the top today. Nor were there any skiers or snowboarders on the well-groomed slope, or basketball players on the painted concrete courts. There weren't boxers in the ring, or soccer players on the artificial turf fields. There weren't any gymnasts or go-kart racers, either.

The emptiness was uncanny, and it made no sense.

The entire Tomas stronghold was deserted. Other than the constant, eerie buzz of the sirens, it was as quiet as a ghost town.

CHAPTER 9

Amsterdam, Capital of the Kingdom of the Netherlands

Any hotel that included *hagelslag* as part of its breakfast buffet was top notch in Dan's book. The chocolate sprinkles were apparently a breakfast staple in the Netherlands.

Dan scooped up a second helping and dumped the sprinkles on top of his buttered bread. "This totally needs to catch on, like, everywhere. I mean, who wouldn't want to eat chocolate for breakfast?"

Cara smiled, but Ian was brooding. "I specifically requested rooms with canal views. My window overlooks a building site. The bathrooms are tiny, the tea is weak, and don't get me started on thread count."

Cara whipped her head around to face Ian. "Right. Because when the levees fail, and the entire hotel is submerged under water, the thread count on sopping wet sheets is *really* going to matter."

Suddenly, the table for three felt rather cramped. Dan stood up abruptly, taking his slice of bread with him. "I think me and my chocolate sprinkles will go for a walk, maybe check out the flood prevention systems on the canals. It couldn't hurt to start scoping things out."

Team A, as Dan had decided to call Ian, Cara, and himself, was starting its hunt for the sabotaged levees in Amsterdam. Being the capital and the most populous city of the Netherlands, it seemed a likely choice for the Outcast to target.

As Dan wandered the streets and polished off his *hagelslag*, he soaked in the sights and sounds of the capital. Amsterdam was absolutely brimming with life. Honking horns, the whir of bicycle pedals, the voices of flower vendors hawking buckets of brightly colored tulips, and boat engines puttering up the canals filled his ears.

It was one of the most awesome cities he'd ever visited. In fact, with all its energy and salty, humid air, it reminded him of one of his other favorite cities by the sea—San Francisco. Like San Fran, the buildings here were slim and towering with colorful, eye-catching facades. The gables on the narrow houses were steep and pointed. Some were made of intricately carved stone, and others had scalloped cornices.

As Dan immersed himself in the city, he noticed that the Dutch language wafting through the streets was husky and full, and that the Netherlanders seemed hardy, helpful, and courteous, as well as remarkably tall. Or maybe they just seemed staggering in height because they had so much to be proud of. A quarter of the country was actually below sea level. The Dutch had battled the sea for every inch of their land for centuries and, so far, they'd come out on top.

A great sinking weight fell in the pit of Dan's stomach. He couldn't fathom the magnitude of devastation that water rolling through the city would cause. He pictured a violent surge crashing in, lapping at the gables of the soaring buildings and entangling bicycles, boats, vehicles, people—everything—in its foaming wrath.

A short section of the Outcast's poem came back to him.

The Gateway floods when autonomy fails,
The torrent erases the Dutch king's trail.

If the levees failed here in Amsterdam, the torrent would erase more than the king's trail. It would erase history and culture, and so many lives—the way Katrina had in New Orleans.

Dan thought the key to stopping the levee failure might be buried in this particular couplet. It was the most confusing, but perhaps the most laden with clues as well. "The Gateway floods," for starters. There were a whole bunch of gateways in the Netherlands—places where the North Sea's entrance was regulated—not just one specific channel or entry. So why had the Outcast capitalized the G in *Gateway*?

And the word *autonomy?* Autonomy basically meant the same thing as independence. Even though

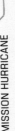

the Netherlanders had a king—some dude named Willem-Alexander—he wasn't a dictator or anything. His role was more symbolic than political. Dan couldn't see how something like freedom could cause a flood in the first place.

The "king's trail" part wasn't helping, either. From what Cara had gathered on the Internet, the king wasn't some aloof monarch holed up in a castle somewhere. He traveled all over the country and didn't have a set route when he did so. Had Willem-Alexander walked down this very sidewalk?

Dan took in the busy streets again—the pedestrians, the cars, the bicyclists. He scanned all the boats on the canals, the people sitting inside cafés, and those heading in and out of museums. He wanted to scream out an evacuation order from the high gabled rooftops. But he still had no idea when and where exactly the attack would occur. Not to mention *how.* It was, as the weather forecasters had predicted, a bright and sunny, storm-free day.

More than half of the country was at or below sea level. And the North Sea was hungry to reclaim its territory. One little breach, and . . .

Dan decided the best he could do for now was focus his attention on waterways leading into the area. But there were *so* many. One hundred and sixty-five *grachten*, which Dan learned was the Dutch word for canals, infiltrated Amsterdam in a complex, weblike system. Not that the city was short on defenses or anything. A ring of big earthen dikes circled the entire perimeter. Just one of the dams alone, the Afsluitdijk, was twenty miles long.

Overwhelmed, Dan took a seat on a nearby bench. He had to think. *What would Amy do if she were here?* When they'd said their good-byes, she'd still been in a funk—all cut up about their grandmother. The whole business of Grace ordering the assassination of their grandfather had really gotten to her.

It made him question his own feelings. Sure, he'd loved Grace. She'd taught them things, taken them to interesting places, bought them ice cream—but that didn't mean she was beyond reproach. Amy's memories of Grace were a lot to live up to, and Dan knew that the two of them always fell short in Amy's eyes. She thought they'd never be as sharp and skillful as Grace when it came to leading the Cahill family.

But with everything that had come to light, Dan thought he and Amy were actually doing a pretty decent job, especially compared to the previous generation of Cahills. Even if they weren't as cunning as Grace, at least he and his sister tried to take a higher road. He and his sister were *always* trying to do the right thing. He wasn't sure the same could be said for Grace.

Dan's gaze wandered to the museum just across the street. *That's what Amy would do if she were here*, Dan thought. Amy would want more information, and what better place to find it than inside a museum?

Dan paid the entrance fee and picked up an exhibit guide. Unfortunately, there wasn't an exhibit titled

"How to Prevent a Flood Disaster Sprung by an Angry Outcast from the Past," but there was one on the history of the Netherlands that sounded promising. Dan headed to the second floor.

He blew past most of the exhibit, but it was clear that floods were as intertwined with the history of the Netherlands as backstabbing was with the Cahill family.

The country was built on a flat river delta, and all the windmills were originally used to pump water out and expand areas of land. Yet all the water they extracted was constantly threatening to come back in.

Dan stopped at some old photographs with a sign above them that read:

They showed houses ravaged by a storm, a frightened horse belly-deep in water, and people rowing boats through flooded streets. The most haunting was of a child and his mother, tears in their eyes and faces sagging with misery, as they both stared at something not captured in the photo.

From what he could gather, *watersnoodramp* literally meant "flood disaster." More than half a century before Katrina, a similar storm tide had overwhelmed the Netherlands' sea defenses. Homes and roads were destroyed and many people were caught unaware when the dikes were breached and the water came pouring in. Eerily, there had even been approximately the same number of fatalities—around 1,800—in both of the storm surges.

Dan balled his fists. They had to stop the Outcast. They had to stop history from repeating itself yet again.

A few feet down from the photographs of massive flooding were photos of the Delta Works—the Netherlands' response to the 1953 catastrophe. Dan tried to wrap his mouth around some of the names of the dams and barriers: Markiezaatskade, Veerse Gatdam, Grevelingendam, Maeslantkering. Even more impressive than the names was the amount of land the barriers protected.

According to the sign, the Delta Works was one of the Seven Wonders of the Modern World. It was said to rival the Great Wall of China.

Dan's stomach turned over. Finding the sabotaged levee wasn't going to be like finding a needle in a haystack. It was going to be like finding a needle somewhere on a forty-acre farm.

He left the history exhibit feeling even more overwhelmed than before. In fact, when he saw a sign for a special exhibit on weapons of mass destruction, he took a detour. Maybe Ian had been right. Maybe their best bet was to go nuclear on the Outcast before he had a chance to strike again.

Dan checked out photographs of mushroom clouds and nuclear submarines. He walked by a model of an aircraft called the B-52 Stratofortress—a jet-powered, strategic heavy bomber. *Now, that's what we need.* The heavy bomber could level the house in Attleboro and the Outcast with it, no problem.

Then Dan came across a sign that read BROKEN ARROWS, and his blood stopped pumping in his veins. His throat went dry as he read the placard.

A ***broken arrow*** is a military term used to describe an accident in which a nuclear weapon is detonated or lost. Up to fifty nuclear warheads went missing during the Cold War. Many of the warheads were lost at sea when submarines sank or airplanes collided.

Dan's blood started pulsing again—too quickly. He almost couldn't think through the pounding in his head.

What if the Outcast hadn't been referring to the Cahill kids when he'd mentioned broken arrows in his riddle? Maybe he'd been talking about nuclear warheads that had gone missing. If the Outcast had recovered one, could he be planning to detonate it underwater?

Dan tried to picture what a nuclear bomb exploding in the North Sea would look like, and the image hit him like a wall of water. It didn't matter one iota that the weather patterns were clear.

Who needs a hurricane if you have a do-it-yourself tsunami-bomb?

CHAPTER 10

Mount Fuji, Japan

Running into a burning building. Hopping aboard a sinking ship. Entering a recently vacated Tomas stronghold while the sirens were still blaring. They all seemed on par with one another.

Sammy bent down near the rail of the balcony and picked up a stainless-steel thermos. Tipped on its side, the thermos appeared to have been carelessly discarded as someone fled the stronghold.

He unscrewed the lid and a puff of steam rose in the air. "This coffee is still warm," he said. "They haven't been gone for long."

Nellie beamed at him. "Nice deduction skills!" she said. "Let's go see if we can figure out *why* they left."

Sammy screwed the cap back on and dropped the thermos.

"Great," Nellie said. "There's nothing up here to shed any light on the mystery. If there is an explanation for this mass exodus, and for what the Outcast is after, we'll find it on the lower levels. Ham said that's where all the offices are located. Now, how are you at skiing?"

Sammy's face broke into a crooked smile. "Nah. I'm gonna shred it instead."

"Snowboarder, eh?" Nellie raised an eyebrow. "You surprise me."

While Nellie strapped on a pair of skis lying near the top of the chairlift, Sammy slipped on a pair of snowboarding boots and buckled into the bindings of a board. In one fluid movement he popped into the air and took off zigzagging down the slope.

"No way are you beating me to the bottom," Nellie whispered to his wind, and then shot into the air herself.

Impressively, the Tomas seemed to have hollowed out nearly a third of Mount Fuji for their stronghold. And they certainly did ski slopes right. Half pipes, rails, moguls, and jumps littered the trail, and the snow machines kept the grounds covered with powder. While Sammy was carving up the white stuff, Nellie streaked past him in a straight line. She would've beaten him to the base anyway, but she couldn't resist—the biggest jump was calling her name.

Nellie flew over the lip of the jump with so much speed that she didn't stop catching air until she landed on the artificial turf that butted up to the ski slopes.

Sammy caught a frontside spin on a rail and then came to a quick backside stop just short of the turf,

kicking up a spray of powder. "Crunchy landing! You got killer steez," he called.

"Skis?" Nellie asked.

"No, *steez*. It's a cross between style and ease." Sammy did a rapid shuffling of his arms, then crossed them over his chest, and again said, "Steez!"

Nellie chuckled. "I must remember to have you sweet-talk me with your snowboarding lingo later. Right now, we need to find some answers."

According to the map Ham had drawn for them, the meeting and surveillance rooms were one level down from the bottom of the ski slope. As they wandered room to room, they found long conference tables, buzzing fluorescent lights, half-eaten pastries, more lukewarm coffee, and computers with screen savers of Mount Everest, the North Pole, and Machu Picchu.

They did not find a single Tomas. Nor was there a fire in the kitchen or anything else that would have constituted an emergency.

"Did you ever sneak inside your elementary school on a weekend, you know, when no one was around?" Sammy asked.

"Beyond creepy, right?" Nellie said.

"Just like this."

"I still don't get it. Why did they all leave?" Nellie asked.

Sammy placed his hands against the far wall of the final room to be checked. He began walking, trailing his fingers along the bricks as he went. "Hold on.

There has to be more to this level. The stronghold seems to expand along with the mountain as we get closer to the base. Yet this level—what we've seen of it, anyway—is smaller than the one above."

"So what you're saying is there's a hidden room or something?" Nellie said excitedly. Perhaps Hamilton hadn't divulged *all* the Tomas secrets.

"Exactly. We just have to find the entrance, and I'm guessing it's somewhere in this room. Notice anything different about this wall?" Sammy asked, still running his hands across it.

"I don't know. It seems more fortified, maybe. The bricks—there's a line in them that shouldn't be there."

Sammy's face lit up as his thumb caught on a groove in the brick unlike the others. "Looks like my batch of ballistics gel wasn't a waste after all—I just found another scanner."

Sammy pulled the synthetic thumbprint back out of his bag and placed it on the camouflaged pad. Immediately, the bricks separated at the line and a secret door swung open directly in front of them.

Nellie grinned. "Sammy, you have steez."

CHAPTER 11

Boston, Massachusetts

Hamilton was in stitches—clutching his stomach and rolling around on the hotel room floor, laughing. "What were you doing making those ridiculous faces?" he asked. "Practicing for selfies?"

Jonah turned beet red, but didn't answer.

Amy cleared her throat to hide her own laughter as the clip of a duck-lipped Jonah reciting Shakespeare to a mirror played on Hamilton's computer screen. The soliloquy Hamilton had traded to the paparazzo for his camera had gone viral. It was popping up every-

where on the Internet—appearing in memes and being spoofed by other stars and wannabe stars alike.

Hamilton hit the REPLAY button and the onscreen Jonah, with one hand over his heart and the other holding the mirror, recited:

> "'The man that hath no music in himself,
> Nor is not mov'd with concord of sweet sounds,
> Is fit for treasons, stratagems, and spoils;
> The motions of his spirit are dull as night
> And his affections dark as Erebus:
> Let no such man be trusted. Mark the music.'"

Ham clicked on the REPLAY button a second time. "It's just too good. We gotta watch it again."

Jonah dropped his head in his hands and groaned.

"You two go ahead. I have to get going," Amy said. "The reading of Aunt Beatrice's will is starting soon."

"You don't, um, want us to come with you, do you?" Jonah offered, picking up his head long enough to look Amy in the eye.

Amy considered. "No, Aunt Beatrice could be . . ." She trailed off, searching for the right word. She finally settled on, "cruel. This reading could be torture. No need for all of us to suffer."

"True that," Jonah said, sitting up straighter and speaking over Hamilton's laughter and his own voice playing in the background. "This is torture enough, yo." He gestured at the image of himself projected on the screen. "If you really don't mind, I think I'm just gonna lie low for a while. Wait until the world finds a new pincushion before I show my face in public again."

"No worries," Amy said.

"Text if you need us," Ham replied, tearing his attention from the screen for just a second before turning back. "Bro, look! This new meme is a mashup of your mime moves in Greece and your mirror time. They're calling it 'Jonah Wizard's Massive Mime Mirror Meltdown.'"

Hamilton sobered up for just a second, almost looking remorseful. "I'm sorry, man." But then he lost it again, breaking into another fit of laughter. "It's going to be eons before the world forgets something this awesome."

There wasn't a screen set up in her great-aunt's formal living room for the reading of her will. That didn't surprise Amy. Aunt Beatrice always got in the last word, but it was also her way to operate underhandedly.

She never would've masterminded a challenge, or recorded herself prior to death the way Amy's grandmother had.

Memories of the day Grace's will was read came flooding back. Amy had been nothing more than a scared little girl when she'd seen the image of her grandmother flicker to life on screen, daring the group to risk everything in a race for power and treasure. The younger Amy never would've believed where the race would take her. That one day she would actually be the capable young woman that Grace had dared her to become.

Amy's anger had oscillated back to sorrow. Thinking about Grace was painful today, like gingerly poking her tongue against a sore tooth.

She canvassed the crowded living room. Had any of the people greedily eyeing her aunt's worldly possessions actually liked the old bat? It seemed more probable that they were clinging to some small hope that they'd been included in her will. Money had a way of attracting flies. So did power. Amy knew that now.

Whoever all these people were, they didn't appear to be family. Even Beatrice's brother, Fiske, had been too ill to show up. *I'm the only Cahill in the room*, Amy thought. That would really irk Aunt Bea.

The majority of the people present were strangers to Amy. But she did recognize Mr. Berman standing at the back of the room, wearing a dark suit and highly polished shoes. Amy's face tightened in anger.

What was he doing here? The butler was tall and big-boned, without any extra meat on him. He also seemed to have a bad case of the jitters. Amy stared him down until he turned to face her.

He obviously recognized her, too. His Adam's apple rippled down his throat as he swallowed hard, and beads of sweat materialized on his forehead.

Amy narrowed her eyes threateningly and shook her head. He swallowed again, then loosened his tie.

You think your tie's too tight? Just wait until I get my hands around your neck.

Amy took a step forward, then stopped herself. What was she doing? Here she was, thirsty for violence, when she'd found the same behavior so shocking in Grace.

Fortunately, Mr. Smood started speaking then, keeping her from dwelling on the matter. "Please find a seat, everyone." His velvety voice rang through the room. "We'll get started in just a few minutes."

Mr. Smood had reserved a seat of honor for Amy at the front of the room. The last thing she wanted, however, was to sit with her back to the butler. Instead, she waited to see where Mr. Berman was going, then claimed a chair directly behind him.

A woman wrapped in furs occupied the seat next to hers. When Amy sat down, the woman glanced over inquisitively, revealing a suspiciously smooth forehead and abnormally full lips. On the other side of the woman sat a man with a restless leg and bad hair plugs.

Amy turned her attention to Aunt Beatrice's collection of porcelain cats lining the shelves around the room. The cats' painted-on eyes and unnatural smiles were undeniably creepy. But studying all their eerie faces was far better than staring at the butler's greasy comb-over.

"Aren't they adorable?" the fur-wrapped woman seated next to her whispered. "How much do you think the collection is worth?"

Amy shrugged. She knew for a fact that Aunt Beatrice wasn't discriminating when it came to shopping for her feline knickknacks. She bought every single kitschy cat she could lay her hands on. Some of them had been picked up from the drugstore, and had come with bright discount stickers adhered to their sides. Yet the woman next to her was eyeing each and every one as though it might be a priceless artifact.

"I'm not sure, but I know that Aunt Beatrice valued them over everything else she owned," Amy answered honestly.

The woman raised her penciled-in eyebrows and smiled a stark white and leering smile. "Bea was your aunt?"

Amy nodded politely, then to discourage any further conversation, whipped out her phone. She flipped through apps aimlessly until the seats were filled, and Mr. Smood quieted the room by raising his hands and clearing his throat. "Thank you all for joining us today in honor of the late Beatrice Cahill," he started. "I must say I am surprised to see so many of you here, as the number at the memorial service was not nearly so large."

"Not nearly so large" was probably being generous. Amy wondered if anyone other than Mr. Smood had made an appearance at her great-aunt's funeral.

Aunt Beatrice had been alone when she died, with only her ceramic cats to witness the murder. Now her family was neglecting her memory after death.

Amy's resentment softened. She felt a twinge of loss and a healthy serving of guilt. That was, until she heard her aunt's last words.

CHAPTER 12

Amsterdam, Capital of the Kingdom of the Netherlands

"Let me get this straight," Ian said, pacing the carpeted floor in Cara's hotel room. "You think the Outcast is going to explode a nuclear warhead in the North Sea so the surge will overcome the levees?"

"Yeah, something like that," Dan said. He'd made it back to the hotel in half the time it had taken him to get to the museum. "Topple, overcome, overtop, breach—whatever. Hurricane or no hurricane, a giant surge of water is blasting through. The important part is: It could happen at *any* time. We can't sit around, twiddling our thumbs, *or* fighting about thread count, while we wait for a storm to blow in."

Ian's face reddened. He looked ready to blow a gasket, but he ignored Dan's comment about bickering over sheets. "Is it possible, Cara?" he asked. "Can't you search that up or something? Posthaste. We need to know if a nuclear explosion can cause such a devastating event."

"All nuclear explosions cause devastating events," Dan grumbled under his breath.

Cara turned to her computer and began hitting keys. "Here's one!" she said, and Ian and Dan gathered around her. The footage was black-and-white and grainy. The first few seconds showed only a few ships bobbing on a peaceful ocean. Then a massive pillar erupted from the water, as if a sea god had shot a fist into the sky. Dan was dumbstruck as he a watched a clip of a four-hundred-and-forty-foot-long cargo ship, docked too close to the testing site, get totally engulfed by a wall of water. His body went rigid—half with fear, the rest with frustration. The video was giving them a clear, horrifying visual of what was coming. But they still had no idea how to stop it.

"I've seen pictures of mushroom clouds over the desert, but I had no idea they tested bombs in the ocean, too," Dan said solemnly.

"Unfortunately," Cara said, "during the nuclear arms race, over a thousand nuclear tests were performed by the United States alone. Most were exploded in secluded areas, like the deserts of Nevada or New Mexico, but about a fifth of them were tested in the atmosphere, underwater, or in space."

"So my question is," Dan said, "should we try to find the bomb and somehow stop it before it goes off, or do we make sure the surge barriers are going to hold? I mean, what if there's some sort of nuclear fallout? Even if we stop the breach, isn't the radiation going to be just as bad? Maybe worse?"

After a few more strokes to the keyboard, Cara said, "I don't think so. There seems to have been terrible radioactive fallout from the tests conducted on land, but listen to this. . . ."

Cara paraphrased what she'd found for the rest of them. "A nuclear bomb was exploded in the Pacific Ocean five hundred miles southwest of San Diego, California. This test—Operation Wigwam—was conducted in 1955, and scientists found that the radiation effects were negligible. Apparently, water dilutes radiation."

"But take a look at that surface surge," Dan said, staring with disbelief at the picture on the screen. "So, I think it's safe to say that the biggest danger is the sea breaching the barriers after the blast, right? Because so much of the Netherlands is already below sea level, it's going to be way more susceptible to flooding than San Diego."

"And the Outcast won't take any chances," Ian added. "He'll explode the bomb somewhere closer than five hundred miles off the coast so as to maximize the effects of the surge, right?"

Cara nodded her head. "Right. I say we still focus our attention on finding the targeted barrier and making sure it holds." Her eyes flicked to Ian. "But it's not my call," she said quietly.

Dan spun around to look at Ian, too. In that moment, he didn't envy their current leader one bit. On one hand, they could try to nip the disaster in the bud and prevent the explosion that would cause the water to surge. On the other, they could focus on the barriers themselves—ensuring that the Netherlands was indeed fortified enough to withstand a raging and violent sea.

Either was a terrifyingly daunting task. Dan gritted his teeth against his growing frustration. They still didn't know which of the numerous barriers would be targeted. Nor did they know where along the 451 miles of coastline the bomb would explode.

Ian ignored their stares and continued pacing the floor of the hotel room, looking as though he had the weight of the world on his shoulders. In a way, he did.

"Maybe we could split up," Dan offered. "You and Cara can rent a boat and some scuba gear, and try to locate the nuke. What sort of broken arrow do you think the Outcast found? A bomb that got lost when planes collided? A sunken nuclear sub? I guess that part doesn't matter. . . . I'll start with the largest surge barriers and inspect them one by one. It'll take a while, but maybe we'll get lucky. Maybe we still have some time."

Dan could tell by the grimace on Ian's face that he'd struck a nerve. Apparently, he wasn't the only one who'd discovered new information to share.

"What?" Dan said, feeling his skin prickle. "What haven't you told me?"

"While you were at the museum, I spoke with the concierge—" Ian said.

"Harassed, is more like it," Cara cut in.

"I merely wanted to find accommodations more suitable to our needs, and it's a good thing I did," Ian said defensively. "Otherwise, I wouldn't have found out that the entire city is booked for the King's Day celebration. In fact, hotels all across the Netherlands are booked for King's Day. It's the biggest public festival of the year."

"And get this," Cara said. "Everyone flocks to the streets, parks, and canals, wearing the color orange in honor of the Dutch royal family—the House of Orange. Sound familiar?"

"As in, 'The House of Orange will crumble and fall,'" Dan moaned. "The attack is going to happen on King's Day. Please tell me that it's *at least* a week away."

Cara and Ian shared a worried look before answering together. "It's tomorrow."

CHAPTER 13

Boston, Massachusetts

Aunt Beatrice had lived her life spewing spite. What Amy didn't know was how much venom the old woman had held back for distribution after she was gone.

The family lawyer slipped a finger inside his collar and tugged, just as Mr. Berman had a few minutes before. "Beatrice Cahill left specific instructions for how we are to proceed," he said, almost croaking out the words. "She requested that those present remain silent, and that no one be allowed to leave until the reading is over. So please, no matter how, er, ugly, this gets, do not vacate your seats."

Whatever Amy's aunt had said in her will—it was bad.

Murmurs of confusion rippled through the room, but curiosity won out. No one protested. When the room once again fell silent, Mr. Smood said, "Thank you. I will now begin.

"'I, Beatrice Cahill, a resident of the Commonwealth of Massachusetts, being of sound mind and memory, do hereby declare this to be my Last Will and Testament.

"'Item One: I give and bequeath to my neighbor, Sophia Fairchild'"—the fur-clad woman sitting next to Amy scooched forward in her seat, her full lips parting to once again reveal her bleached white smile— "'absolutely nothing. You weren't expecting that, were you, my dear?'" Mr. Smood read. "'Oh, how I wish I could be there myself to witness that plastic smile of yours being wiped clean off your face.'"

Amy cringed as the woman's jaw indeed fell, gaping open. Mr. Smood's eyes flicked to the woman, full of pity, but he continued reading nonetheless. "'Don't think I didn't notice what you were hinting at every time you complimented me on my silk scarves or commented on my lovely china settings.

"'I am not vapid, you know, although, I cannot say the same for you. As for your husband, he could certainly use a new fedora or a good herringbone cap to cover up that monstrosity of a hair transplant, but I will not be the one paying for it, if that's what you think.'" The man sitting next to Sophia Fairchild withered in his seat.

"'Item Two,'" Mr. Smood continued, and what followed was a slanderous attack directed at Beatrice's hairdresser.

"'Beth Moorgate, you are a hopelessly unfashionable woman with no scissor skills whatsoever. Whatever possessed you to entertain the thought of

beauty school in the first place, I cannot imagine.'"
Sitting two rows ahead of Amy, a young woman wearing Crocs, a plaid skirt, striped knee-high socks, and gold hoop earrings covered her face with both hands.

"'Ms. Moorgate, to grant you any inheritance would be ludicrous. If anything, you should be paying back my estate the money I spent on that dreadful perm.'"

The woman began to tremble behind her hands, and Amy was hit with a wave of compassion.

Item Three was a general denouncement of anyone who continued to patronize the corner store on Washington and Third Street. Beatrice said the shopkeeper there had once treated her in an "undignified manner." If Amy recalled correctly, the man had accused her aunt of shoplifting when she accidentally dropped her handbag and no less than a dozen ceramic cats came spilling out.

The barrage persisted, with Aunt Beatrice slamming everyone in the room with varying degrees of insults without bestowing anything of any value to anyone. It appeared her aunt had asked Mr. Smood to gather them all here merely to dish out one last verbal lashing.

"'Item Twenty-Three: As for my great-niece and -nephew, Amy and Dan Cahill . . .'" Mr. Smood paused, pinning Amy with a sympathetic look, and she braced herself for the onslaught she knew was coming.

"'Being charged with your care and upbringing was by far the worst thing that ever happened to me.

Dan, you were such an uncouth child, and ever unapologetic for your ill-mannered ways. Sadly, you were beyond reform by the time you were placed in my custody.'"

Amy burned with anger. *Thank goodness you couldn't get your claws in him!* she thought.

"'Amy, I had hoped that one day I might turn you into a highly regarded member of café society. Wouldn't that have been marvelous?'"

Um, no. Amy had zero interest in living the life of a socialite. She'd always been far more interested in history and the world than being seen at the trendiest clubs. *I hate the spotlight.*

"'But you hated the spotlight,'" Mr. Smood read. "'In fact, all this attention is probably making you uncomfortable right now. I can just see your face turning that unattractive red.'"

Aside from the crack about Dan, Amy had been doing just fine up until that point. But when the audience turned to look, blood did in fact rush to fill Amy's cheeks. It made her so angry she could feel hot tears gathering behind her eyes.

"'Even worse than being shy, you proved to be as ruthless and cruel as your grandmother before you.'"

The scorch of embarrassment transformed into something more. Shame. Maybe, deep down, Amy feared she was on course to becoming every bit as ruthless as Grace. Perhaps she already was.

"'Now, I have heard the whispers that I am nothing more than a bitter and disagreeable old woman. To that

I say, hogwash.'" The crowd tittered and even Mr. Smood looked as though he was restraining a chortle.

The absurdity of Bea's words reeled Amy back in. It reminded her just how batty and self-absorbed her aunt had been to the very end. The heat drained from Amy's cheeks. *Nothing that woman says is going to touch me again.*

"'I want everyone to know that if there is an ounce of truth to these accusations it is only because my heart was shattered by these insolent children. I have never fully recovered from being tasked with their guardianship. Amy and Dan, neither of you will receive a single dime of inheritance money.'"

Mr. Smood finished reading and glanced in her direction. He was clearly measuring her reaction with his gaze. Amy rolled her eyes to let him know that she was fine. Aunt Beatrice had been bitter long before they ever came into the picture. And they certainly didn't want any of her money.

The lawyer let out a tiny puff of air and smiled warmly at her before moving on to the next item.

"'Item Twenty-Four: Not a one of you knows how difficult it has been to hold my tongue all these years.'"

At this, Amy slapped a hand to her mouth to keep a laugh from escaping. When had Beatrice Cahill *ever* held her tongue? But the laughter died in her throat as Mr. Smood went on. "'I have been forced to stand by while the idiocy of family and friends (primarily family) has caused me great strife. However, I did find small comfort in recording the wrongdoings in my extensive diary collection.'"

Aunt Beatrice kept diaries?

"'My diaries provide important documentation of the Cahill family history and should be treated in a manner worthy of their value. Therefore, it is my last request that they be added to the Cahill Library at Attleboro.'"

Mr. Berman shot up from his chair. Amy glowered at the back of his head. It was now blatantly obvious why he was here. Whatever the Outcast was trying to hide by killing Aunt Beatrice might have been recorded in her diaries.

"Please take a seat, Mr. Berman. I'm not finished," Mr. Smood said curtly.

"I'm sorry. I'm . . . I'm . . . not feeling well." The butler clutched his stomach and moaned unconvincingly. Then he pushed his way down the row of people, tripping over legs and purses as he went.

Amy whipped her head around. *Snake! He's going to look for the diaries!*

Amy considered following as he broke free from the room and disappeared up the staircase. But the man was an idiot. Even if he did manage to locate Beatrice's diaries, there was no way Amy was letting him leave with them. It was kind of nice to let someone else do the legwork for once.

While the lawyer moved on to the next item, Amy discreetly pulled out her phone once more. She

punched in three lines of text for Hamilton and Jonah:

```
MEET ME AT AUNT B'S STAT
LOOK FOR GRACE'S GHOST
DON'T LET THE BUTLER LEAVE
```

Mr. Smood droned on for another fifteen minutes, reading Aunt Beatrice's sometimes trivial, sometimes bizarre requests. Occasionally, Amy would hear a rustling noise upstairs. Either Bea had done a halfway decent job of hiding the diaries, or else Mr. Berman was even more inept than he looked.

At last, Mr. Smood came to the final item. "'Item Thirty-Seven: Let there be no further speculation. I am leaving the entirety of my estate, all liquid assets as well as those that can be auctioned off, to be used as funding for the Porcelain Cats Are People Too Foundation, and for a museum which will be erected in my honor and which will house my beloved and enviable collection of ceramic felines.'"

The room gasped, but Amy couldn't help grinning. You had to hand it to Aunt Beatrice—her parting shot was a good one. Amy leaned over to the woman sitting next to her. "You know she had more than twenty million dollars, right?"

The woman broke into tears. "Come on, Harold," she sniffled, smearing mascara across her face as she dabbed her eyes with the sleeve of her shirt. "We wasted ten years buttering up that dreadful old woman; we're not going to waste a minute more of our time on her!" With that, the couple stood and marched out, giving Amy a free path.

The grumbles of a disappointed crowd muffled the noise from the upper level, but Amy had kept one eye on the staircase throughout the will reading. Mr. Berman was still upstairs. While everyone else filed out of the house, Amy went to find him.

The second floor had been ransacked. Books littered the hallway and the furniture had been upended. Aunt Beatrice would've left explicit instructions for where to find the diaries with Mr. Smood. Amy knew she could probably just ask him where the diaries were. But her Great-Aunt Beatrice was dead, killed in cold blood by Mr. Berman's employer. And even as nasty as Beatrice was, Amy wasn't about to let the butler go without a little bit of payback.

She bypassed her great-aunt's bedroom—where the mattress was askew and the closet had been raked—and followed the trail of disarray to Bea's study. Mr. Berman glanced up, sneered at her, then went back to rifling through a file box.

"Too obvious," Amy said, and walked out.

The only upstairs room not disheveled was the bathroom. And in it was one detail jarringly out of place. Mr. Berman came up behind Amy, standing so close she felt his hot breath on the back of her neck.

"The bathroom? You've got to be kidding me," Mr. Berman said.

"It's been a long time since Bea had a *living* cat in her house," Amy said. She reached down for the kitty litter box positioned next to the toilet. The butler threw himself over her back. They collided in the space between the bathtub and the porcelain bowl, and Amy gave a last-minute jab of her shoulders that sent Mr. Berman flying. She pushed aside the litter box and pulled up the trapdoor hidden beneath it. Amy yanked out a surprisingly large and surprisingly heavy wooden box. She could see stacks of leather-bound journals between the box slats. Mr. Berman scrambled back. He snatched a glass perfume bottle from the vanity and squirted it in Amy's face. The overwhelming artificial scent of roses flooded the room, as if the ghost of Beatrice had returned with stinky vengeance for both of them.

Amy dropped the box to grab a towel. By the time she'd wiped her eyes, the butler and the heavy box of diaries had escaped down the staircase. Amy rushed after him, taking the stairs two at a time. She made it outside just in time to catch a glimpse of the butler skidding to a halt on the curb in front of Grace's shiny Rolls-Royce Ghost.

Jonah was leaning against the luxury sedan. A hideous fake mustache and dark glasses obscured most of his face. Next to him Hamilton, in his usual athletic garb, waved jovially at Mr. Berman.

The butler spun around just as Amy caught up. She flashed him a prickly smile.

"Oh, forgive me for being so rude. Amy Cahill, isn't it?" he said, now trapped between the three of them. He glanced from one Cahill to the next, pausing slightly longer on Jonah's mustachioed face. Then he broke into a soft chuckle. "Jonah Wizard. I suppose you think that I am 'the man that hath no music in himself, let no such man be trusted' and all that."

"Yeah, and I'm the man that hath no patience," Hamilton deadpanned.

Mr. Berman's face fell. "Well, to be honest, the diaries aren't really my thing. I far prefer green paper to parchment. If you catch my drift?"

"What? You want money in exchange for the diaries?" Ham turned to Amy. "First the paparazzo and now this scumbag? I don't know about you, but I'm fresh out of Franklins *and* embarrassing Jonah clips."

Encroaching on Mr. Berman's personal space, Ham cracked his knuckles loudly. But he backed off when an elderly woman leaving Aunt Bea's shouted, "Is everything all right, young man?" She shook her cane at them. "Is that teenager getting all up in your grill?"

Hamilton looked back and forth between Mr. Berman, who wasn't anywhere close to being a "young" man, and the old lady who'd obviously wasted too much time on YouTube. His eyes finally came to a rest on Jonah. "What do you say, Wizard? You're the one with deep pockets."

"No way," Amy said as Jonah reached for his wallet. "I've had enough of money-hungry people for one week. I can handle the butler."

Whipping her leg up and around in one smooth circular motion, her kick stopped just shy of Mr. Berman's windpipe. "Hand over the diaries, or next time I won't hold back."

The butler swallowed hard and carefully set down the box of diaries. Jonah scooped it up. "Easy-peasy, yo. Like candy from a baby," he said.

"I'm calling the police!" the old woman screeched.

Amy dropped her leg, and Mr. Berman immediately raised a hand to his throat. As he massaged his bulging Adam's apple, he snickered.

"What's so funny?" Amy asked.

"You may have the diaries," the butler scoffed, "but you'll never see your cat again."

Amy's heart sank like a stone and she gasped.

Mr. Berman smiled maliciously at her response. "I dumped Saladin at a shelter on the way here and asked them to dispose of him as soon as possible. He's most likely receiving a lethal injection as we speak."

Two things happened at once. Amy didn't hold back as she whirled her leg through the air a second time, and the old lady jabbed Mr. Berman squarely in the gut with her cane. The end result was the butler lying flat on his back, wheezing and clutching his stomach.

"Never mind," the old lady clucked in her phone. "My eyesight is going. I must have dialed the wrong number." After she hung up on the police, the woman gave Mr. Berman another jab with her cane before climbing into a car with a CRAZY CAT LADY bumper sticker and driving away.

"We've got to find Saladin!" Amy yelled as she lifted the keys from Mr. Berman's suit pocket. As she slid into the passenger seat of Grace's luxury sedan, Amy was already searching shelters on her phone. Ham took the wheel and Jonah jumped into the backseat, and they sped off.

There were a total of three shelters between Grace's house in Attleboro and Aunt Bea's house in Boston. Amy furiously dialed the number for the first. "Did anyone turn in an Egyptian Mau today? Black spots, frisky attitude?" Amy asked as soon as her call was picked up. "No? Okay." *Click.*

Bile was rising in her throat, and her heart pounded in her ears as she dialed the next number.

"Where am I going, Amy?" Ham asked as he swerved around a slower moving vehicle.

"Head west," she answered, but changed her mind after striking out with the second shelter as well. "Make that south. Sorry."

"One shelter left," Hamilton said, and Amy nodded gravely. "Enter the GPS coordinates before you make the call." Ham cranked hard on the wheel and the Ghost went up on two tires as he took the next corner without touching the brakes.

Come on! Come on! Come on! Amy fought panic as she waited for someone to pick up on the other end of the phone. Instead, the call went to a messaging service.

"Our normal business hours are nine A.M. to five P.M.," the recorded voice said. Amy glanced at the clock on the dash. It read 5:01. Her phone hand dropped limply to her lap.

"It's closed for the night," she said, her voice hollow and disbelieving.

Tightening his jaw, Ham cast a sidelong glance at her as he took the next turn. He looked back at the road just in time to slam on the brakes. Traffic was at a standstill and flashing lights indicated an accident.

"Hold on," he said, throwing the sleek sedan into reverse. Amy knew he'd aced a course in defensive driving, but her heart still hit her throat when he kicked the car back into drive, then veered around the brake lights and onto the shoulder.

Amy gripped her armrest, scanning for medical personnel or onlookers. She didn't see any people in their way, but what she did find was even more alarming. Her heart skipped a beat as Hamilton stomped on the accelerator and the car careened toward a tow truck pulled to one side of the road.

The truck's flatbed was lowered and they sped like a bullet straight for it. Ham didn't let up on the pedal as they raced up the steel ramp, blasted over the tire blocks, and went airborne.

The surreal trip over the cab of the tow truck stole Amy's breath away. The next instant, her teeth were rattling and her bones jarred as the Ghost landed, then shuddered back to life on the pavement.

"What are you doing, Hamilton!?!" screamed Amy.

"I always wanted to try that," Hamilton said. He was grinning like a maniac as he cut in front of the wreck and peeled back into the driving lane.

When the Ghost at last screeched to a stop in front of the shelter, Amy flung open the door and bolted for the small brick building.

She pounded the windows with her fists.

When her friends caught up with her, she was almost in tears. "What if he's already . . ." Amy couldn't bear to finish that sentence, so she started a new one, her voice cracking as she said, "How am I ever going to break the news to Dan?"

"Yo, we're not giving up that easily, are we?" Jonah said, then plastered his face to one of the windows. "Dude, there's a light on in back. Help me make some noise."

Hamilton nodded. "Oh, yeah, it's Hammer time."

They beat the glass so hard, Amy feared it would break. "Let us in!" the three kids screamed in unison.

To Amy's surprise and relief, an employee entered the dimly lit corridor. Amy wasn't as happy about the peeved expression on the woman's face. She glared at them through the glass, lifted a solitary finger, and pointed it at the CLOSED sign.

"Hey, bro," Hamilton whispered to Jonah, "you're up."

"Nooo," Jonah groaned. "Not again."

"Totally. You gotta play the celebrity card. If not for us, do it for Saladin."

Jonah reached up with both hands. With one, he ripped the ridiculous handlebar mustache from his face. With the other, he tore the tinted glasses from his eyes.

Recognition hit the shelter employee like a Mack truck. She staggered backward a few steps, her eyes wide with excitement, before nearly tripping over herself as she rushed to unlock the door.

"Jonah Wizard!" she said breathlessly. "I had no idea it was *you*."

Up close, Amy could see that the woman was barely older than the three of them—fortunately, an age well within Jonah's fan demographic.

As the young woman self-consciously fidgeted with her uniform and dealt with a wayward strand of hair, Amy pushed her way past.

"Wait, you can't go back there!" the woman yelled, but Amy was already halfway down the hall. Trying not to notice how cramped the cages were or how the animals cowered in the corners, she charged from room to room, searching for Saladin. Her panic flared each time she came to a cage and her cat wasn't in it.

She checked four rooms before coming to one with a sign that read EMPLOYEES ONLY. Without hesitation, Amy burst through the door.

A scowling employee stood in one corner, holding a pointy syringe. His face was marred by a puffy red scratch. Blood trickled down his cheek, and one entire sleeve of the man's uniform was shredded. "Help!" the man whimpered.

There was a loud hiss and then a silver ball of spotted fur soared through the air and clamped onto the man's pant leg. The man yelped. He shook his leg, but Saladin's teeth and claws were sunk deep and guttural rumbles were rolling out of the cat's mouth.

"Saladin?" said Amy.

The cat abruptly changed his tune. He delicately detached four legs from the man's pants, sauntered over to Amy, and with a graceful leap, was in her arms.

Amy stroked Saladin's gleaming fur and nuzzled her face against his back. Throat closing and knees nearly buckling, Amy gave one giant sigh of relief. "Oh, Saladin, you poor thing!"

"What?" the man shrilled. "Are you serious? *I'm* the poor thing!"

Hamilton and Jonah burst in, eye-daggers trained on the man with the pointy syringe whimpering in the corner. "That cat is pure evil!" the man shouted.

"Let's get out of here," Amy said, still snuggling Saladin. "If we hurry, we can probably make it to the fish market before it closes. Red snapper, here we come."

Once Saladin had devoured a healthy helping of red snapper and was curled up cozily beside her on the hotel bed, Amy cracked open Beatrice's diaries.

Jonah, reading over her shoulder, groaned in disgust. "Ugh. Listen to this part: 'My daily beauty routine appears to be paying off. Everyone says I'm as stunning as any Hollywood bombshell. I cannot argue, as I've been blessed with a complexion to rival Bette Davis's and shapely lips that even Joan Crawford would envy.'"

"Sounds like important Cahill documentation to me," Hamilton said, unable to keep a straight face.

Amy smirked—she couldn't argue with his sarcasm—and kept flipping through the journals. The first diary contained entries ranging in date from when Beatrice had been in her late teens to her early twenties. Most of the accounts were viciously told. Beatrice's resentment of her younger siblings, Grace and Fiske, was painfully clear.

Amy read an entry dated shortly after Fiske was born:

I am still in a state of shock and utter disbelief. How is it possible that my dear mother could have traded her life to bring such a vile creature into this world? The infant does nothing but wail all hours of the day. It is his own fault that no one but Grace comes to soothe him—he, who has ended all brightness for the rest of us.

Father has left. It has fallen on me as the oldest to name the unwanted child, and I have decided upon the name Fiske—an Old Norse word for fish. I will not lie; it is with sweet vengeance that I have settled upon this name, as fish are something that I thoroughly detest.

Amy resisted the urge to pitch the journal across the room. She had left Dan in serious danger for this? To do nothing more than read her aunt's worthless vitriol?

Her frustration mounted as she scanned several more entries in which Beatrice lamented life with a newborn brother. Then she found one about Grace that gave her pause. Granted, the diary only contained Beatrice's side of the story, but it did make Grace sound rather vindictive.

Fiske remains quite irritating, but recently Grace has proved to be the very bane of my existence. Everyone else seems to find her spirited temperament quite charming, but they haven't seen the calculating, vengeful side of her willfulness, the way I have.

For weeks now, I have noticed an odor when applying my facial cream at night. I am quite diligent about skin-care, but I will not digress . . . The pungency of the cream became quite unbearable, at times even interfering with my sleep. However, I was reticent to dispose of the cream as the bottle was nearly full and very expensive.

It was only late last evening that I discovered the source of the stench. When I returned to the powder room to fetch a bobby pin, I discovered Grace adding several drops of fish oil to my night cream. I can only presume that she is still cross with me for picking such a name for our brother, and I suspect that she has secretly read the reason I chose it for him. Needless to say, I will need to find a better place to conceal my diary. . . .

Amy's stomach churned with worry. Once, she would have thought Grace's prank was funny. But was this an early glimpse at a darker, more menacing side of Grace? It was one thing to pour fish oil in your sister's facial cream, but something else entirely to put a hit on your estranged husband. Wasn't it? What if Grace hadn't known where to draw the line?

It wasn't until Amy had browsed through two more journals that she found what she was really looking for—Beatrice's account of Grace's marriage to Nathaniel Hartford.

"Okay, I think this is it," she said.

Saladin mewed, but no one else responded. By then, Hamilton and Jonah had already faded. Amy had no idea at what point they'd fallen asleep.

She kept reading. It was difficult to weed through Beatrice's ramblings and retellings, but it was clear that Beatrice had been jealous of how young and in love Grace and Nathaniel were when they wed, poised to lead the Cahill family. Where things went sour wasn't quite as clear, especially when every passage was tainted by Beatrice's spiteful viewpoint.

However, one entry stood out:

I'll admit, my relationship with Grace has been strained, to say the least, but it's certainly not for lack of trying on my part! Why, just this evening I invited my sister and her husband to dine at my home. Was Grace even appreciative of all the trouble I went to in contacting the caterer and making certain the maid thoroughly cleaned the house before they arrived? I should say not!

She squabbled with her husband the entire time. From the moment she stepped through the door, she was irate. Nathaniel stormed in after her. "It's not like the Ekats aren't already using the latest technology to keep tabs on all the other branches," he said.

I politely offered to take their jackets, but Grace ignored me. She spun around and fired back, "I know where you're heading with this. I know you, Nathaniel! This is just the first step for you in establishing total control."

Personally, I like the idea of being able to snoop on family members without their knowing. Just think of all the juicy gossip I could capture!

While the kitchen staff passed out hors d'oeuvres, I voiced this opinion and, oh, how Nathaniel grinned at me. That man has charisma in spades.

The look on his face was not nearly as charming, however, when he turned back to Grace and said, "Just because you don't agree with my tactics, don't fool yourself into thinking that we're not after the exact same thing."

I'd like to point out that this is the very reason I never get involved in Clues matters. In my opinion it's all too bothersome.

Grace glared at her husband and had the audacity to say, "I may want the same thing as you, Nathaniel, but I will never sink to your level to get it."

Ah, the drama. I certainly do not condone their behavior, but what a thrill to witness such an ugly quarrel!

For a second something very dark crossed Nathaniel's face. If I didn't know better, I'd almost have thought Grace looked afraid. "You've sunk to my level and beyond it," Nathaniel replied. "What about your black files, Grace? Did you think I don't know about those?"

After that, Grace clammed up and the night was ruined! We spent the rest of the evening eating beef Wellington and my favorite carrot-and-lime gelatin mold in silence.

That was it. Bea's account of the evening cut off there. That her grandparents had been hunting for the 39 Clues was old news to Amy, but the black files certainly piqued her interest. They sounded important. It sounded like, with them, Grace was compiling information on all the Cahills. Did that mean she'd kept one on Nathaniel, too? Did she spy on her own husband? Amy swallowed.

Amy quickly scanned through the diaries a second time. She skimmed for any hints as to where Grace may have hidden the files but came up empty-handed. Asking her aunt was obviously out of the question, and there was only one other person she could think of who might be able to tell her: her Great-Uncle Fiske.

Amy flipped open her laptop. Saladin saw the action as an invitation to prance across her keyboard.

He purred as she nudged him aside and then dialed Fiske's number for a video chat.

When her uncle answered the Skype call, two things became immediately clear. One: Her call had awoken him. Two: He'd relapsed since she'd last seen him.

Instead of the healthy glow he'd sported after his first few months in Mexico, his skin was pallid. And his cheek and collarbones protruded as though he'd lost a significant amount of weight.

"Sorry to bother you, Uncle Fiske," Amy said, forcing her lips into a smile. She didn't want her face to betray how much his deteriorating state upset her.

"No, my dear! Don't be silly. It's never a bother to chat with you. I'm afraid I nodded off in my hammock, but I'm fully awake now." Amy had never known Fiske to be unfriendly. Sometimes it was hard to believe that he and Beatrice were even related—or that he and Grace were siblings, too.

"Tell me, how did the reading of the will go?" Fiske asked. "It's a pity I wasn't up to being there. Although, I must admit, Beatrice never had a kind word for me. I can't imagine anything—not even death—could've changed that." An expression of deep sadness flit across her uncle's face. "What a terrible end to an unhappy life."

Beatrice had included some words in her will regarding Fiske, but not a single one of them was worth repeating. "Oh, she really didn't have much to say . . ." Amy hedged. "But I did manage to get ahold of her diaries today, and I found something in them that I'm hoping you can assist me with—something that might help us to identify the Outcast."

"Of course, I'll help in any way I can," Fiske said. Then he succumbed to a fit of coughing.

She wasn't sure how much she should tell her uncle. He didn't know about Grace's kill order. Part of Amy wanted to share the secret just because she knew he'd make an attempt to set her mind at ease.

Fiske had idolized Grace. Maybe he could reassure her that his sister had been the wonderful person Amy always thought she was. But no matter what kind of front Fiske put on, the news would rattle him. His health couldn't take that. She could protect him from the knowledge of Grace's murderous intentions, but she couldn't protect him from everything if she was going to find the files.

"Aunt Beatrice wrote about Grace keeping black files on all the people in her life," Amy said, watching for her uncle's reaction.

Fiske hesitated, then nodded his head.

"You knew about them?" Amy asked incredulously.

He averted his gaze. "It wasn't something Grace was proud of. But, yes, she confided in me about the files. She was recording all the feuds and any secrets she thought might be useful somewhere down the road. It was how she determined who was fit for high-ranking positions and who wasn't, how she kept some people in line, and how she justified casting out certain members of the family. It's likely that she kept one on the Outcast—whoever he is."

Amy thought she knew. But for that huge of an accusation, she needed confirmation. "Do you have any idea where to look for the files, if they still even exist?"

Fiske rubbed a hand across his sallow face. He seemed to be considering a long list of possibilities. At last, his eyes darted back to Amy's. A smile lit up his pale face and he said, "Whenever Grace was stuck on a problem, or on how to settle a family dispute, she always went flying. She always came back with her most daring and devious solutions."

"You think the black files might be at her private airplane hangar?"

"Yes, I do." Fiske nodded.

Amy felt her face stretch into a smile, too, only to have it fall a second later. Grace's hangar was in Attleboro—deep within Outcast territory.

CHAPTER 14

Boston and Attleboro, Massachusetts

After hanging up with Fiske, Amy checked in with Dan.

"So we think the Outcast has a broken arrow that he found and fixed somehow," her brother said. To anyone else, the wobble in his voice would have passed unnoticed. "And he's going to detonate the nuke tomorrow during this huge national outdoor party. When the spray hits land, he's literally going to rain on the Netherlanders' parade. Can you believe it? That Outcast is one demented old dude."

Amy's breath caught in her throat. She felt a throbbing knock against her rib cage. "Dan." She whispered his name like a lifeline tossed across the ocean that divided them. "You can't stay there. You have to go."

The smile on Dan's face dissolved, allowing her to catch a glimpse of the fear he'd been trying to mask. "I can't leave," he said. "All these people, this beautiful city."

Saladin must've recognized Dan's voice. He meowed plaintively in the background.

"Whoa! Please tell me that was who I think it was." Dan bounced back to life on screen.

Amy pulled herself together for Dan's sake. She caught him up to speed on what was happening on her end and stopped asking him to vacate the Netherlands. As much as she wanted him to be far away from the danger, she knew her brother. He would never walk away.

A bolt of shame speared her. Was she just going to accept the risk to her brother's life? Perhaps she was as ruthless as Grace. But what other options were there? Ian was smart, capable, and strategic, but the pressure of leadership was getting to him, causing him to make mistakes. The Netherlanders needed someone who also possessed tried-and-true instincts.

They needed Dan.

"I can't believe we're this close to Grace's house—make that *your* house, Amy—and we can't even stop in for a snack or to use the toilet," Ham said as he slid back in behind the wheel of the Ghost.

"I know, right? Gas station bathrooms stink. Literally," Jonah said. "Why do you think I'm holding it until we reach the hangar?"

"Whatever, man, it was worth it. Now I can sit in comfort while I eat my Funyuns." Hamilton cracked open the bag of onion-flavored rings that he'd picked up inside the convenience store.

"Not while you're driving, you can't," Amy said, snatching the bag from his hands and tossing it into the backseat with Jonah.

Jonah scooped it up and started munching on the rings.

Glancing back at him in the rearview mirror as he pulled out of the gas station parking lot, Hamilton cried, "Hey! Leave some for me."

Jonah took another ring out of the bag and popped it in his mouth. "Consider this payback for the Shakespeare clip." His eyes narrowed. "Payback number one, that is. You're not getting off that easy."

Within minutes, they were pulling up to a large grassy field surrounded by a high-security fence. Amy held her breath as she punched in the code to open the gate securing access to Grace's private hangar and airstrip. She half expected the numbers to set off an alarm and for Grace's luxury sedan to be swarmed by a fleet of armed guards. When the light turned green on the keypad and the Ghost rolled through the gates, she let her breath out.

The padlock on the hangar door was a different story, however. It took every trick Amy had learned from her lessons with an old cat burglar, but a good fifteen minutes later they were in. Amy's breath caught in her throat again.

The hangar reflected more of her grandmother's personal tastes than any room back at the estate. Grace had once told Amy that flying was the one thing that made her feel most alive. The goggles Amelia Earhart had worn when she became the first woman to fly solo across the Atlantic were stored in a glass cabinet atop a marble stand. A model of the Wright brothers' *Flyer I* hung from the ceiling. Tacked to the wall beneath the *Flyer* was a black-and-white photograph of the first flight. It was even autographed by Wilbur and Orville Wright.

The hangar felt like a museum honoring Grace and her deepest passion. When Grace was alive, she'd kept the place spotless. Seeing the layer of dust coating everything now affected Amy more than it should have. Grace had been gone so long now. Those happy afternoons Amy had spent here with her grandmother felt so achingly distant. But the layer of grime over everything felt almost deserved after how tarnished Grace's memory had become.

Back when she and Dan had been hunting for the Clues, all Amy'd had to do was think like her grandmother, and most often, the solution would present itself. Locked box? Ancient riddle? No problem. Amy would draw inspiration and courage by imagining Grace's presence beside her, helping her along.

Now when she listened for Grace's voice, all she heard was silence. And she wasn't sure she wanted to keep her grandmother's memory so vividly alive after all that she'd learned. But Amy did want to find the black files, even if she was afraid of what they might contain.

"Where did you hide them, Grace?" Amy whispered as she peered around the hangar, trying to see past her memories.

Her eyes swept across the concrete floor and landed on her grandmother's plane. It had been draped with a tarp. "Help me uncover the *Flying Lemur II*?" Amy asked the boys. They stopped looking around and sprang into action, tugging the drab gray sheet off Grace's plane.

The *Flying Lemur II* was painted a cheery yellow color. Grace had commissioned someone to custom-build an exact replica of the old-fashioned original. Fancy oriental rugs that Grace had collected from her travels were spread beneath the propeller plane's wings, and an aircraft tug was parked just in front of it. The airplane may have looked antique, but the tug—the tractorlike vehicle used to guide the plane to the runway—was cutting edge.

While her friends ran upstairs to the loft, Amy walked the perimeter of the plane. There wasn't much in the way of things to be rifled through. The hangar was spacious and uncluttered, with mostly plush creature comforts upstairs—a padded sofa and a kitchenette—and aviation memorabilia downstairs and hanging from the rafters. When she heard the refrigerator door creak open in the loft, Amy called out, "I'm pretty sure Grace didn't keep the files in her freezer."

"What?" Hamilton answered. "Jonah ate all my Funyuns and I'm still hungry."

Amy was revolted. "Don't forget to read expiration dates!" she called back.

The files weren't in the fridge, and Grace hadn't kept a single filing cabinet on the premises. Amy was starting to fear that Fiske had been wrong.

Perhaps Grace had hidden the black files back at the estate, or even somewhere else. She had houses and hiding spots tucked away around the world. Maybe Cara could find a way to hack into Grace's bank records and see if they'd missed a safety deposit box in her name. Amy clenched her teeth in frustration. Dan was on the other side of the world staring down a tsunami, and she was on a cold trail. Still, she couldn't resist climbing into the cockpit of the *Flying Lemur II*. She wasn't sure she'd ever get another chance.

She gripped Grace's control wheel and placed her other hand on the throttle lever. For a minute, she let good memories wash over her—flying over rolling green fields and gazing out at endless blue skies. Amy had thought her grandmother to be the best and bravest woman in the world. She wished she still felt that way. Tears prickled against the back of her eyes. *It's like she died again*, Amy thought.

As Amy was about to hop out of the plane, something the Outcast had said came back to her. He'd been quoting Grace at the time, his image projected on the screen in Grace's own house as he vied for control of the family. *If your best instincts are your worst enemies, take your hands off the controls. Find someone else to fly the plane.*

The Outcast had twisted the meaning of Grace's words in order to use them against the younger generation of Cahills. He'd claimed that the Cahill kids were amateurs, untried and unfit to lead. That the family should find someone else, meaning the Outcast, "to fly the plane."

Grace may not have been the person Amy thought she was, but she couldn't imagine her grandmother ever thinking like that. She was always the first one to take charge of a situation, and she'd encouraged Amy and Dan to do the same—to assess their surroundings and do what needed to be done. *Take your hands off the controls. Grace, what are you really saying?*

Then it hit her. She was sitting in the wrong place. Amy bolted out of the pilot's seat and over into the copilot's position. She felt under the seat. She looked for anything on the dashboard that didn't fit and ran her fingers along the underside of the control panel. Sure enough, her racing fingers found their mark—a small button hidden from view.

Amy pressed it, her expectations high. But nothing happened. She pressed it again. Still nothing. Disappointed, she shook her head and climbed out of the cockpit.

What a waste of time.

"Let's leave before the Outcast realizes we're here," Amy called up to her friends. They started down the stairs as Amy moved toward the front of the plane.

When she reached the end of the rug, it buckled beneath her.

"Amy!" Jonah cried in surprise. "Are you okay?"

Amy had fallen to her knees on the unstable ground. She quickly rolled to one side, then pulled back the Persian rug. Pressing the button had worked after all. It had activated a hidden door. Amy gaped through the open hole at a staircase plunging into darkness.

Alek Spasky stewed while he sat hidden by a thicket in the woods just beyond Grace Cahill's hangar. He regretted not hitting at least one of the children with his emei piercer when he'd had the chance.

If Alek had maimed just one of them before they'd entered the hangar, it would've made the wait far more bearable. Granted, the Outcast had ordered him to hold off until the children led him to the files. But the Outcast wouldn't begrudge Alek a little fun in the meantime, would he?

As it was, he was nothing more than an overpaid babysitter. The thought galled him. He was tired of lurking in the shadows, when today was supposed to be his day to rise. Alek's right hand, his spear-hurling hand, twitched.

Watching a video feed from inside the hangar, he noticed that Amy had climbed into the cockpit of the plane. Hate and loathing ate at Alek like acid. He longed to make her suffer.

The Cahill girl took bold steps with all the self-assurance of an older sister. Alek's own sister, Irina, had operated the same way. He'd spent most of his life trying to impress her. Trying to prove himself worthy of her love and attention.

Alek had been following in Irina's footsteps when he joined the Komitet Gosudarstvennoi Bezopanosti— the machine that was the KGB. But Irina had treated him with disinterest as she outshone him in every manner and rose to the top of the secret spy agency. She'd been cool and aloof, bestowing him with nothing more than an indifferent smile when he finally attained the highest rank alongside her.

Irina had been ice.

She'd never cared for him, never shown him any softness. And any hint of feeling in her had died with her son. But perhaps her coolness was a blessing in disguise. Her rejection finally caused Alek, too, to turn away from his family. And when he did, he found something extraordinary. Until the hubris of the Cahill family took it away from him.

And for what?

Then Irina went and threw her life away, too. One moment of tenderness, and it was wasted on the Cahill children.

They had cost him too much.

Today Amy and Dan would atone for two lives cut short, for acts of kindness imparted on the undeserving. They would pay him back with blood.

The media would speculate on the origin of the nuke in the Netherlands and which terrorist group was responsible for its detonation. True, it had been the most brilliant, tinkering Ekaterina minds that had made the bomb operational once again, but without Alek none of it would have been possible.

Alek would make sure the entire world knew that he was responsible. He would contact the media himself. He'd need his own alias, of course. How about "the Steel Rod Assassin"? No, that was ridiculous. It was far too long and comic-book-sounding. Unlike "the Outcast," which was all at once threatening and concise. Alek's own father had been called "the Scalpel." Could his alias be "Son of the Scalpel"? No, that also was horrendously long.

Alek would have to give it more thought. He'd meditate on it after he dealt with the children. Glancing again at the video surveillance, he noticed Amy clambering back out of the cockpit. *Boring*, Alek thought. Then she stumbled and pulled back the rug. When he saw the hole that had opened up in the floor, he smiled.

And so it begins.

CHAPTER 15

Attleboro, Massachusetts

The worst traps in life are set by the ones we love.

Amy and her friends cautiously descended the steps leading into Grace's underground bunker. The stairwell was narrow and the darkness enveloping as they dropped deeper into the earth. "Be careful," she warned Hamilton and Jonah. "I don't think this clue is one Grace ever intended us to find."

"Would now be an okay time to mention that your grandmother always freaked me out?" Hamilton said.

"Me too," Jonah confessed. "Grace was wicked smart, but you never knew where you stood with her. One day she could be lavishing you with compliments, and the next she'd be serving your head on a platter to the rest of the Cahills."

Amy bristled and goose bumps rose on her skin. She sucked in cool air only to find that it was stale and musky, like that of an ancient tomb. How had her perception of Grace been so far off the mark? Had everyone been able to see what she'd apparently missed?

Once her foot connected with the bottom step, Amy heard a loud *click* and the door above them quickly glided shut. Completely blinded by the darkness, Amy swallowed the urge to scream.

Instead, she charged back up the steps and frantically felt for a button or a release lever for the door. There wasn't one—much like the outside had been, the inside of the door was entirely smooth—a solid, sliding panel.

They were trapped.

A wave of claustrophobia washed over Amy, but she heard a buzz and a light flickered on.

"Found a switch," Ham reported as Amy made her way back to the bottom landing. She blinked her eyes, adjusting to the fluorescent overhead lights.

"Thanks, Ham." Now that the corridor was illuminated, Amy once again took the lead.

A series of framed photographs hung on the thick concrete walls. Starting with the Wright brothers' first flight, it seemed to be a time line of aviation. Each photograph was hung in precise alignment except for a black-and-white photo of a jet fighter. The jet fighter was hanging slightly askew.

Jonah reached out to straighten it, and Amy's arm instinctively shot up. She caught Jonah's hand a millisecond before it landed on the frame. "Don't touch it," she said. Her voice sounded cutting even to her own ears.

"Why not?" Jonah asked.

"Something doesn't feel right. Give me a minute to think."

"A lot doesn't feel right to me," Hamilton muttered.

Jonah dropped his hand to his side and Hamilton meandered farther down the corridor. The hallway ended in a sharp turn. Not one of them could see what was beyond the corner.

Amy stared at the photo. A faded memory was being pieced together. Grace had swatted her arm away from a crooked frame once. "Don't ever do that," Grace had warned. Then she'd taken Amy to an air museum and shown her a plane just like the one in the photo. It was a Messerschmitt—Me 262—the most common fighter jet used by the Germans in World War II.

"It's a trap," she told Jonah. She repeated the story her grandmother had told her. "During World War II, German engineers rigged crooked picture bombs to target high-ranking officials. They hollowed out walls and set explosives behind pictures in abandoned buildings. The pictures were left crooked, and then when Allied forces set up shop in the buildings and someone straightened the frames, it tripped the bomb and everyone nearby was killed."

"Whoa. So you're saying that Grace's bunker is, like, booby-trapped—that we need to watch out for trip wires and stuff like that?" Jonah shook his head. "That's trippin', yo, in more ways than one."

"Maybe not trip wires exactly, but motion—"

Just then, an alarm sounded and a faint, sweet odor filled the air.

Hamilton came barreling back around the corner. "Oh man, I activated some—" His head slumped forward and his body followed. He hit the floor. Hard.

"Ham!" Jonah sprang ahead, but Amy yanked him back, her arm nearly wrenched out of its socket.

"We can't!" Holding her breath, she pulled her shirt collar over her mouth and nose and indicated for Jonah to do the same. They ducked close to the ground, watching Ham's limp body for signs of life. He never so much as twitched.

Be okay. Be okay. He has to be okay.

The wait was agonizing, but the saccharine scent eventually left the air. They rushed to check on him.

"Do you think he's all right?" Jonah asked worriedly.

Amy lifted Ham's head and pressed her fingers to the carotid artery just left of his windpipe. "I don't know," she said, but she picked up a slow beat and some of the tension left her shoulders. "But at least he still has a pulse." Perhaps Grace wanted to merely incapacitate intruders—not kill them. The realization might have been reassuring if it wasn't overshadowed by one clear fact: Hamilton was hurt because he'd been caught in one of Grace's snares.

Jonah breathed a heavy sigh of relief. "What are we going to do with him?"

Amy glanced around. "I think we have to leave him here. He's too heavy to take with us." After gently laying her friend's head back on the cement, she stood up. Every nerve ending in her body was on high alert as she and Jonah inched around the corner Hamilton had cleared.

The hallway opened up into a larger room entirely crisscrossed with laser beams. At the back of the room, a sizeable black safe was embedded in the concrete wall.

Jonah turned his head to look at Amy, his eyes bulging. "Are you kidding me?" he said. "There's gotta be some serious dirt in those files."

"There must be a way to shut the lasers off," Amy said. "Look for a panel."

"Yeah, let's just not bump any picture frames while we're at it," Jonah mumbled. Amy could barely hear him over the sounding alarms.

It didn't take long for Amy to locate a keypad on the wall. It consisted of both numbers and letters. But what if it was another trap? If she entered the wrong passcode, she and Jonah could end up in the same boat as Hamilton. Or worse.

Full of dread, her fingers shook as she punched in the address for her grandmother's estate. They weren't the right keys, but at least a pendulum blade didn't swing out from the wall. She tried the address for the hangar next, followed by Saladin's name and his birthday. Then she did the same for herself, for Grace, and for Dan. She tried her parents' names and their wedding anniversary.

With the alarms pounding in her ears, it was extremely difficult to concentrate. What else could she try?

Then she knew.

She hit N376S, the tail number she'd just seen printed on the *Flying Lemur II*.

Nothing.

Amy shook her head, ashamed of her own stupidity. Whenever Grace retold the story of how the original *Flying Lemur* had crashed, she'd grumbled about the one thing that couldn't be replicated exactly. The *Flying Lemur II* had to be given a unique tail number; it couldn't legally be registered under the same one that had been painted on its predecessor.

Amy had never personally laid eyes on Grace's first plane, but she had noticed a photo of a bright yellow propeller plane hanging with the other framed pictures in the corridor. She blew past a bewildered Jonah, back around the corner, past Hamilton—still collapsed on the floor—then found what she was looking for near the end of the hall.

When she returned to the keypad and punched in N237W, the ringing stopped. The laser beams shut down. The door to the safe swung wide open.

CHAPTER 16

Mount Fuji, Japan

The vault door was ajar. The hulking form of Magnus Hansen stood hunched in front of it with his back turned to Nellie and Sammy. He was blocking their view of what lay inside.

Before Nellie could think to question why the Tomas leader would be breaking in to his own branch's vault, he rose to his full, formidable height and swung around. He turned his ice ax on Nellie and the expression on his face was emotionless—as stone-cold as his gray-blue eyes.

Nellie gasped, grabbed Sammy protectively, and looked frantically around for a tactical position, for a way to defend themselves from the machinelike man towering before them. Her eyes caught on the bag at Magnus's feet. They'd interrupted him as he was pilfering items from the vault. Interestingly, the rugged tunnel carved into the side of the mountain was littered with Super Bowl rings, expensive medallions, and gold trophies. But the items poking out of Magnus's gym bag—a fresh, fleshy leaf from an aloe plant, a human femur, a quartz crystal the size of a baseball—were not ones that your average person would expect to be secured deep inside the heart of a stronghold.

A tingle ran up Nellie's spine and the hairs on the back of her neck stood on end. She wasn't your average person.

Nellie took a step backward, nudging Sammy along with her. "The clues," she said, her voice ringing with accusation. "You're stealing Tomas clues for the Outcast, aren't you, Magnus? It's never been about the disasters. The disasters are just a distraction!"

Magnus continued to stare at her blankly. Nellie knew that in his eyes, she wasn't a threat—just a pesky fly to be dealt with when she swarmed too close. *Good.* She could use that to her advantage. She took another step back and kept talking.

"The Outcast made you leader of the Tomas for this very purpose, didn't he? So you could force an evacuation of the stronghold. The 'punishing' of the Cahill kids—it's all a cover. The Outcast just wants to keep them out of the way while he steals the thirty-nine clues." Nellie's face grew hot. "Don't tell me he actually plans on using the serum."

Still no reaction from Magnus, even though Nellie knew she'd hit on the truth. One thing didn't fit, though, and Nellie found herself wondering out loud. "But why didn't you have the combination to the lock on the vault? Why the ice ax?"

Magnus's iceberg eyes narrowed almost imperceptibly.

Then Nellie remembered something else she'd heard about Magnus. He'd had some financial trouble with the Tomas treasury. He'd been kicked out of the family for some conspiracy that Grace had uncovered years ago. It wasn't until the Outcast reinstated him that Magnus had once again become active in the Tomas network.

"They didn't trust you, did they? The rest of the Tomas—they didn't trust you with the combination, even though you're their leader."

Without warning, Magnus charged like an angry bull. An angry bull with an ax. But that's what Nellie had been counting on. She reached back, snagged a heavy marble trophy, and hurled it straight at Magnus's head. A sharp corner of the base caught Magnus between the eyes. He let out a groan and crumbled to his knees.

Nellie screamed, "Go!" and she and Sammy high-tailed back the way they'd come. As she went, Nellie threw everything she could in Magnus's path—medals, trophies, plaques—anything to slow him down. A few steps ahead, Sammy was fiddling with something by the secret entrance. "Come on. We don't have time!" she said.

"Just another second!"

Nellie didn't have another second. Magnus was up and his ax was swinging.

Nellie ducked, narrowly avoiding decapitation. She felt the hairs on the top of her head lift as the ax whistled past and the serrated blade dug into the wall.

The Tomas leader grunted and heaved to dislodge it. The ax came loose. At the same time, Sammy grabbed Nellie by the arm and pulled. She was almost out the door when Magnus lunged after her, clamping his free hand around her boot. Stuck in a tug-of-war between her scientist boyfriend and a former Olympic athlete, her bets were on the athlete.

But she could even the odds.

Nellie twisted, leaned back into Sammy, and raised her other boot. She landed a kick that sent Magnus's head cracking back on his beefy neck. He let go and Nellie went rocketing all the way through the doorway, landing in a pile with Sammy on the floor. Nellie slammed the door shut with her foot. She sprang to a vertical position, ready to bolt, but Sammy didn't get up. He didn't move. He just grinned at her, as if all of a sudden, he wasn't in such a terrible hurry.

"What did you do?" Nellie asked, frozen in midflight.

Sammy's grin stretched wider. "Oh, I just disabled the fingerprint scanner. The one that opens the door from the inside."

"So he's stuck in there?"

A loud *thwack* reached their ears from the opposite side of the door and Sammy's grin faltered. "For now. But he does have an ice ax, the stamina of a horse, and the strength of a polar bear."

Thwack!

"I don't think we want to be around when he eventually chops his way out," Sammy added, hopping to his feet.

Thwack!

"And we need to break the news to my kiddos," Nellie said. "They have to know what the Outcast is really after."

Thwack!

A brick on the false wall rattled, kicking a tiny cloud of dust into the air.

"Yeah. But we can't tell them if Magnus brings this whole place down. Let's go!"

CHAPTER 17

Attleboro, Massachusetts

Hamilton opened his eyes. Amy was sitting cross-legged beside him, the black files scattered everywhere on the corridor floor in front of her.

"Where's Jonah?" he asked groggily.

"You're awake!" Amy said, throwing her arms around him and helping him to an upright position. Her lips curled into a smile, but Ham could see her eyes were haunted and scared.

"He's searching for a way out," Amy continued. "The concrete walls block reception on our cell phones, and no one even knows we're here. Not even Dan."

"I knew you'd find those," Hamilton said, gesturing at the files. His head felt heavy and it was throbbing. When he explored his forehead with his fingers, he found a large, tender bump. He massaged it gently.

"Did I hear Ham's voice?" Jonah said, popping out of the bottom of the stairwell. His face went supernova bright when he saw that Hamilton really was awake. "Dude, you're up!"

"Any luck finding a way out?" Amy asked.

Jonah's face fell. "Nah. Get cozy, homeys. We're stuck here for a while."

Hamilton cast a thin smile to Jonah, then turned back to Amy. "So what did you find out? Anything good?"

"I wouldn't say 'good,'" she replied carefully. She couldn't quite meet his eyes. "Apparently, Grace called them 'black files' because they're full of blackmail material. There's a file here on almost everyone we know. I just . . . I just can't believe Grace did all this. If she didn't have dirt on someone, it seems like she was perfectly okay with inventing it. It's awful."

Amy looked down at her hands, and her voice broke awkwardly. "There's even a file on your father."

"My dad?" Hamilton asked. He wasn't sure he wanted to know.

Amy met his eyes again. "Grace is the real reason he was kicked out of West Point. After Eisenhower forgot the rule about taking guns off campus—"

Hamilton had heard the story before. "Dad was just so excited to show his rifle to my grandfather. He totally spaced out that he wasn't supposed to take it with him when he left West Point to visit his family," he said, his voice rising as he spoke.

Amy nodded slightly. "I don't doubt that," she said. "But maybe you shouldn't look in the file. You might not like what you find."

Hamilton ignored her warning. He had to know. The dark gray folder had the name *Eisenhower Holt* printed in gold on the cover. He took it from Amy, flipped it open, and found a photograph of his dad, dressed in a crisp military uniform, paper-clipped to one side. Below the photo was a student number followed by a grades report from West Point. Someone had stamped EXPELLED across his father's face in bright red letters.

Grace had included a handwritten note:

Despite his temper, Eisenhower is friendly and charismatic. People are naturally drawn to him. If he succeeds in graduating from West Point, I fear he might gain too much favor among the Tomas. Mr. Holt clearly does not possess the intellectual capacity for the important decision-making that may be required of him should he take on a prominent role within the family.

Hamilton set his jaw. He resisted the urge to hit something. His dad wasn't a rocket scientist, but he wasn't a dummy, either. Just because the Tomas were athletically gifted didn't mean they were all a bunch of blockheads.

"I know. I'm sorry," Amy said as though she'd been reading his mind. He could feel her hand hovering above his shoulder, as if she wanted to offer comfort but didn't know where to start.

Hamilton exhaled through his nose as he turned the page.

The Honor Board at West Point has decided to let Eisenhower off with a warning for taking his gun off campus, as it was his first transgression. Therefore I have decided to take matters into my own hands. A fake ID, cheat sheets, and proof of plagiarism have all been planted among Eisenhower's possessions. Conveniently, Arthur Trent is his current roommate at West Point. Thanks to his affinity for my daughter, he was easily persuaded. I have given Arthur clear instructions where to look for the fabricated evidence of honor code misconduct. I have no doubts that once Arthur hands over the items I planted, the Honor Committee will in turn rule in favor of expulsion.

By the time he finished reading, Hamilton's body was rigid with anger. "How dare she?" he said, his voice

THE 39 CLUES

126

quavering with emotion. "My grandfather was framed, too, for allegedly leaking secrets to the Ekats. More than anything, my dad wanted to redeem the Holt family name. He thought graduating from West Point would be the first step."

A hot tear pooled in the corner of his eye and rage boiled in his chest. "Grace stole the opportunity right out from under Dad's feet." His voice broke. "You know, I've always wondered why my dad is so bitter. It's no secret that we aren't really that close. Things might've been different if Dad had graduated, if the other Cahills showed him more respect. Honestly, he has a great sense of humor, but he always uses it to cut me down. Like I'm a huge disappointment."

"I'm so sorry," Amy said. Hamilton watched as blotches of red blossomed on the skin of her neck and cheeks. She was really upset—maybe even as upset as he was.

"That's messed up, for sure," Jonah chimed in. He crossed the room and sat down with them. Ham could see that Jonah was clenching and unclenching his jaw, and something inside him lifted just a bit to see his friends so upset for him.

"Like, what happened to our parents and grandparents?" Jonah continued. "How'd they all turn into such a bunch of backstabbers?"

"Hypocrites," Amy said. "Imposters."

"Slanderers," Ham added, with a dark look at the file.

"I thought growing up was supposed to make you smarter. It, like, has the opposite effect on our family," Jonah said.

Amy nodded her head in agreement. "I wanted to be just like Grace. I wanted to live up to her. And now . . . I just can't believe this. Is *this* what being the leader of the Cahill family turns you into?"

Hamilton sniffled, then reached out for her hand. "No. Not you, Amy. You're better than that."

Amy took his hand and wrapped it in her own. She gave him a wavering smile and squeezed. "I hope you're right," she said. "But I haven't shown you everything that I found."

Hamilton retracted his grasp as Amy picked up another file. She gripped it so tightly that the skin around her knuckles turned white and her hands began to tremble. "The one on Nathaniel Hartford is the most terrifying, and I'm afraid that Grace didn't fabricate everything that's written about him."

The tremble from her fingers overtook the rest of Amy's body, and she gave a sob and buried her face in her hands.

Hamilton and Jonah exchanged a glance. "Amy?" Ham asked.

She lifted her head. Her face was ghost white, and her eyes were clouded with fear. "I'll be all right," she said uncertainly, and cleared her throat. "It seems like Grace and Nathaniel were both obsessed with finding the clues, but Nathaniel's obsession . . . how far he was willing to go to get his hands on the serum.

He . . ." She clutched the file to her chest. "My mother. His own daughter. He threatened to—" Amy said choppily, unable to complete a single sentence. She buried her head again. "It's too awful. I can't."

Hamilton gingerly placed a hand on her back. "It's okay. You don't have to tell us now." He felt her back heave beneath his fingers as she gulped in air and let it out again.

"Thanks. There is one helpful item, though," she said. She sat up straight, wiped her cheeks, and pushed back the hair that had fallen in her face. Hamilton could see the effort it took to force herself to get it together. "The file contains a photo of my grandfather. It's from forty years ago. But if we ever manage to get out of here, we'll run an age progression on it so we'll know what Nathaniel Hartford looks like today."

"And if he's the Outcast, right?" Jonah asked.

"Right. And maybe—" Amy stopped abruptly and they all listened.

A grinding sound echoed from the stairwell. The secret panel was sliding open.

Ham's skin prickled. His tongue felt like a stone in his mouth and his gut tightened. They hadn't done anything to open the door. So who had?

Amy shoved the file into her pack, and she and Hamilton sprang to their feet a second after Jonah.

"What's the plan?" Hamilton whispered. "Whoever opened that door has us backed into a corner. If we stay down here, there's no hope for escape."

A look of understanding passed between the three of them.

"Okay, then." He felt his anger solidify into resolve. No matter how hard the world tried, he wouldn't become the victim his father was. "We dive for cover as soon as we reach the top. Agreed?"

Amy and Jonah nodded their heads. Then the three of them bolted up the stairs together and launched themselves through the opening in the floor.

As Ham ducked and rolled, a small silver missile flew through the air and Jonah let out an agonized shriek. An iron fist clenched around Ham's heart.

"Jonah!" he screamed.

For an excruciating moment, Ham could only see the horrendous way Jonah's face was contorting with pain. He couldn't see where the emei piercer had nailed him. He couldn't tell if the injury was life-threatening.

Reaching back, he encircled an arm around his friend's waist and hauled Jonah along, then dove for cover. They slid to a stop behind the aircraft tug a second later, just as another silver object whizzed by Ham's ear.

As Ham dropped his cousin, Jonah clutched his leg and writhed in pain. Hamilton glanced down at the steel rod impaled in Jonah's thigh and breathed a sigh of relief. *Better there than in his chest.*

"Spasky?" Ham asked as Amy slid safely behind the cover of the tug.

"I didn't get a good look, but it's got to be," she said. "How bad is it, Jonah?"

"Takes a lot more than one spear to do in the Wiz," Jonah joked. But it was obvious by the way his face crumpled and his body folded in on itself that he was suffering.

"If we don't act fast," Amy said, "it might come to a lot more—for all of us."

A great white wave of anger hit Hamilton. Why were some people so bent on making others miserable? He peered over the tug, then whipped back as Alek let another steel rod fly. Ham felt the whoosh of air splitting around him as the rod sliced straight through the spot where his head had just been. The emei piercer ignited sparks as it hit the wall behind them and clattered to the floor.

Fire boiled in Hamilton's veins. His words were knife sharp as he reported back to the others. "Spasky is standing near the hull of Grace's plane. He has enough spears in his pack to turn us all into Swiss cheese."

"Yo, but we have him outnumbered," Jonah said.

Hamilton inhaled, then shot Amy a grim look. "Have any ideas?"

"I do!" Jonah said. "When we were searching for Grace's files, I saw a switch for the fire suppression system on the wall. It's right by the door." He winced again as he pulled himself upright and pointed at a button inside a glass box on the opposite side of the hangar. "If we can activate the switch, the foam might disorient Spasky long enough for us to jet. I went to this foam party once and—"

"Got it. Try not to talk too much, bro. Can you snag that cone behind you?" Ham said. "I wouldn't ask—you know, 'cause you have that, um, spear sticking out of your leg . . ." Just looking at the wound made Hamilton feel light-headed. "But you're the one closest to it."

Jonah grimaced as he reached for the orange traffic cone sitting by one of the tug's rear tires. Hamilton whispered in Amy's ear. She nodded and then took the cone from Jonah's hands.

"On the count of three. One. Two. Three!"

Amy popped out. The sound of another flying rod hissed in the air. Using the cone as a shield, she dropped into the seat of the small tractor, started the ignition, and wedged the gas pedal down with the cone. As the tug lurched forward, Amy threw herself from the vehicle.

The tug caught Alek by surprise. It pinned him to the side of the plane just as Hamilton made a break for the switch.

He opened the glass, hit the button, and instantly the hangar began to fill with thick clouds of fire-suppressing suds.

Alek roared and Hamilton glanced in his direction, then grinned. One of the sprinklers was spraying right in Spasky's face. Beneath the white lather the assassin's skin was beet red. Then the anger in Alek's eyes turned to panic as he was swallowed up entirely by the foam.

The three kids slogged around the spray. Then Ham and Amy helped Jonah hobble out the nearby door. Submerged beneath ten feet of foam, and immobilized between the tug and Grace's plane, Alek Spasky was no longer a threat.

"Huh," Hamilton said, feeling slightly vindicated. "Do you realize we just took down an ex-KGB spy with *bubbles*?"

CHAPTER 18

Amsterdam, Capital of the Kingdom of the Netherlands

On King's Day, or Koningsdag as the Dutch call it, everyone in the Netherlands seemed in a topping mood—everyone except Ian, Cara, and Dan.

Ian's stomach was tied in knots. The view outside the hotel window showed a city awakening and loads of jolly people streaming into the capital. Beyond the glass pane the streets and canals were streaked with orange. People in orange shirts. People in puffy orange wigs. People in orange Morphsuits? *Well, horses for courses,* he supposed.

He, Cara, and Dan had stayed up late into the night researching everything there was to know about the extensive system of storm barriers and dikes in the Netherlands. By all accounts, the technology was first class, and the country was the model for flood prevention. Yet, in Ian's experience, anything powerful had an Achilles heel, a weak spot in an otherwise impenetrable armor. Ian just had to place his finger on the weakness before the Outcast exploited it.

Every smiling face plastered on each passerby only added to the crushing pressure. A smartly dressed, precocious child who reminded Ian a bit of himself was refusing to hold his mother's hand as he toddled down the sidewalk. The child obviously wanted to lead the way.

Being out in front isn't what you imagine, chap. You think it's all about freedom and telling everyone else to step in line. Come to find out, you're the one in shackles.

The concierge had said that close to a million visitors would flock to the already populous city of Amsterdam for the day, and Ian still had no idea which levee the Outcast would target. A small, shameful part of him called out to run before the wave hit. That's the way he'd been raised—to look out for himself above all others. But there was the lovely Cara, and Dan, and all these cheerful Netherlanders to consider.

I'm no longer my own agent, Ian thought with sickening clarity.

"There you are," said Cara. The hand she placed on his arm turned his insides to mush. Perhaps being alone wasn't all it was cracked up to be, either. It hit Ian that every second mattered right now. He might not get another opportunity to tell Cara how he truly felt about her.

"Cara, I have feelings—" He wanted to say "for you," but she cut him off before he could.

"Oh, I know that, Ian," she said quickly. "I apologize for treating you like you don't. It's just that, sometimes, you act so aloof. I feel like I have to go overboard to get through to you. If I hurt your feelings about the thread count and harassing the concierge, I'm really sorry."

"I wouldn't say *aloof*!" Ian objected. "*Sophisticated*, perhaps? But that's not what I'm trying to say. I want you to know—"

"Know what?" Dan asked as he joined them. "What did I miss?" He must have hit the breakfast buffet, he was carrying a piece of buttered bread with *hagelslag*.

Ian watched with a disapproving eye as Dan took a bite. He couldn't very well declare himself to Cara with Dan around.

"What?" Dan said through a mouthful of food. "Can't save the world on an empty stomach."

"I have something to tell you both," Ian said, changing the subject. While they were still sleeping, he'd been channeling his inner Kabra. He may have repressed most of his upbringing, but it had still left its stamp on him. And Kabras specialized in one thing: influence. Whether it was through wealth or a show of strength, or even by blackmail or terror, they bent others to their will. Which was exactly what was needed here.

"I've demanded a meeting with top government officials." Ian turned to Dan. "There are important Cahills all over the world, and I never understood why you and Amy never threw your power around before. But that's beside the point. The meeting is scheduled for nine-thirty A.M. Thirty minutes from now. And it wasn't easy to get. It is, after all, a national holiday." Ian puffed up. "Fortunately for us, nobody says no to a Kabra."

Ian expected at least a small commendation for his efforts. Perhaps even a little affection mixed with wonder from Cara. He had imagined her squeezing his hand, gazing adoringly into his eyes.

But the looks on his friends' faces were questioning at best.

"Do you really think a meeting is a good use of our time?" Cara said, and if Ian wasn't mistaken, there was a hint of accusation in her voice.

"Why do you keep asking me that? You said yourself that we're shorthanded," Ian shot back defensively. "How can the three of us possibly expect to stop a flood of this magnitude? We need resources." He warmed to his theme. "We need military personnel at our disposal. We need a team of experts and emergency response units. We need people doing exactly what we tell them to, and we need them now."

Cara and Dan shared a look that only served to fuel Ian's indignation. They were undermining his authority. He could privately doubt his role as their leader, but they could not. They had to follow his orders without question, or everything would fall apart. How could he ever be the effective leader they needed him to be if they didn't place their trust in his decisions?

"I just don't know if these 'top government officials' are going to respond the way you want them to," Cara said. "They may have agreed to meet with us out of some sort of obligation to the Cahill name, but most adults don't appreciate being ordered around by a group of teenagers."

"When Napoleon Bonaparte set up the Kingdom of Holland to extend French reign over the Netherlands, the Dutch certainly listened to what *he* had to say," Ian shot back.

"Okay," Cara said. "Random much? And I'm pretty sure Napoleon wasn't a teenager at the time."

Wounded by her sarcasm, Ian couldn't help but wince.

Cara noticed and reached for his arm. "I'm doing it again, aren't I? I'm sorry," she said, but Ian brushed her away. "Look. I don't want to hurt your feelings, and I'm not saying we won't try it your way." Cara sighed. "We just need to be prepared for handling the situation on our own if they won't step in. That's all."

Ian turned his attention out the window to a new group of pedestrians, each wearing a bright orange hat and furry orange boots. "The meeting is in one half hour at the Café de Jaren. You are both free to join in, if you'd like. Otherwise, good luck finding the targeted barrier." He gestured at the masses of people outside the window and added, "In that crowd."

Inside the Café de Jaren, the atmosphere was every bit as bustling as it was outside on the streets of Amsterdam. But Ian, Cara, and Dan were led right to a table for six on a lovely terrace overlooking a canal.

Umbrellas provided shade for all the tables. Overhead, the rising sun was bright, and the sky, clear—not a single storm cloud in sight.

Two men in ill-fitting suits with orange ties and a woman in a carrot-colored silk scarf and a bulky navy-blue blazer rose to their feet to greet them. Their fashion sense left something to be desired in Ian's opinion, but he had to give them bonus points for their patriotism.

He shook each of their hands and the woman began speaking with a heavy Dutch accent. Her words sounded full and throaty as she said, "My name is Anki. I am the chairwoman for the city council. Our apologies that the mayor couldn't join us—*Burgemeester* Aldert De Bardelben has other pressing matters to attend to. But we are happy to hear your grievances, granted that it won't take more than ten minutes. As you can imagine, with today's festivities, our council members are already spread quite thin."

"I'm sorry, did you say 'grievances'? We don't have *grievances*," Ian spat out. "This is a matter of national security!"

"Please, take a seat, Mr. Kabra, and help yourself to some tea," the woman said soothingly. "May I recommend the apple tarts? I daresay you won't find better in all the world."

Ian glanced around the terrace. Other diners had dropped their spoons and put down their teacups.

People were staring. Had his outburst truly been that loud?

The only sounds now came from the buzzing traffic and the high-spirited crowds below. He sat down in a huff. When everyone else at their table joined him, the lively chatter and the clanking of silverware again picked up and wafted through the air.

Ian lowered his voice to a whisper and leaned forward to address the government officials. What he had to say would knock the smug looks off their faces. "We have reason to believe that a bomb will explode somewhere in the North Sea. Today. We also have reason to believe that the shock waves from the explosion will breach your surge barriers, causing widespread flooding. With this information, we expect you to do whatever is within your power to prevent such an occurrence."

Take that for "grievances"! Ian thought. He'd practiced this speech on the way over and, by his own assessment, had given it with quite impactful delivery.

"Now," he continued, "you must call in the Royal Netherlands Navy. The air force can give us an aerial view of all the dams and levees, and certainly the larger cities need to be evacuated immediately. We can wait if you'd like to start making phone calls."

"I see," said the woman calmly. She frowned and then turned to the man sitting beside her. "Thjis, what is the daily count for bomb threats in the Netherlands up to?"

The man she'd called Thjis glanced at something on his tablet. "This is only the fourth, but it's still early, Anki."

"Ah, yes, but I'd wager that this is the only threat currently placed against the sea . . . Well, I think we can all rest assured that our flood prevention system is the finest in the world—we Dutch learned our lesson when the 1953 flood broke through the dikes. If that is all, it was very nice meeting you, Ian. You are a credit to the Lucian branch."

"You can't be serious!" Ian balked, once again raising his voice. "I don't care how great you think your system is. It's going to fail."

Anki rose to her feet. "I don't 'think' it's great. I *know* that it was designed to withstand a ten-thousand-year storm. I know that our technology is more advanced than what is found with any other flood prevention system in the world. The Oosterscheldekering is nine kilometers long. It has sixty-five concrete pillars and sixty steel doors. The Maeslantkering, between Rotterdam and the North Sea, is one of the largest moving structures on the planet. It has two gigantic mobile gates that swing into place when a surge is likely. The Netherlands is nothing if not prepared. Now, if you'll excuse us . . ."

The two men rose. They flanked Anki as she started to walk briskly away from the table. "Wait!" Dan called after her. "Please! Do you have any kids, Anki?"

The woman paused a few feet from the table. "A boy and a girl," she answered, turning to face Dan.

"I have a sister," Dan said. "She's not here today, because I have a job to do and so does she. But we'd do

y

MISSION HURRICANE

141

anything to keep each other safe. I bet you feel the same about your kids."

Anki bristled. "Of course I do!"

"Right. Look, I know you have a lot to do and you don't think this threat is legit. But we do. And we're going to do everything we can to keep your boy and girl, and everyone else in the Netherlands, safe. Maybe you can't call in the navy or the air force, but if you give us a few more minutes of your time, it could make all the difference. Please," Dan pleaded again.

Anki glanced at her watch. "I've just enough time for one more question."

"Thank you," Dan said, sounding sincere. "Now, those two barriers you mentioned—the Oyster King and the Meister King—"

"The Oosterscheldekering and the Maeslantkering," Anki corrected.

"Uh, what you said," Dan replied, and Ian rolled his eyes.

What is Dan doing? Granted, that bit about "Do you have any kids?" had regained the idiot woman's attention, but now Dan needed to be swift and exacting instead of making them all seem like fools.

"Yeah," Dan continued. "The steel doors and the giant gates, you said they close when 'a surge is likely.' But how does that happen, exactly? I mean, who makes that call? Is it put to a vote, or is it a single person who does all the deciding—like he or she is operating independently or something?"

Ian flinched. *Autonomy fails*. Perhaps Dan knew what he was doing after all.

"By my count, that was three questions wrapped into one," Anki said, her lips twitching, but she answered him anyway. "People more qualified than I decide when the steel gates of the Oosterscheldekering close. As for the Maeslantkering, the decision is made by a computer. Perhaps you can request a meeting with it. A computer is likely to have far more time available than we do on an important national holiday."

"This computer, it acts independently, then?" Ian blurted.

"You children don't give up, do you?" Anki said, obviously exasperated.

Taking a cue from Dan, Ian forced himself to swallow his pride. "Please. I know I was brash before. I'm . . . I'm . . . sorry." The apology nearly choked him. "But this is important. We need to know if the word *autonomy* can be applied to any other dike, dam, or barrier within the Netherlands' flood prevention system. Or if it's only the Maeslantkering that, with its computer, is self-governing, so to speak."

Anki searched his face as she considered, and Ian kept it straight, successfully resisting the urge to shout, "Think, woman! We haven't got all day!"

"It's a strange question." Anki's answer came slowly pouring out. "But, yes, I would say that the Maeslantkering is the only barrier that operates that way—without any human interference. I suppose you might describe that as autonomy. Now, we really must go. Good day."

With that, Anki spun on her heel and she and the other council members were gone, disappearing through the double doors that led back inside the café.

Cara quickly drew out her phone and began scanning something on the screen. Her face paled. "I don't know how we missed this before. The Maeslantkering's computer monitors the weather and sea data. Then, based on an algorithm that predicts how much the sea level is going to rise, the computer triggers the closer. The massive steel arms swing shut whenever the algorithm says a storm surge is likely."

*"The Gateway floods when autonomy fails—*a computer won't be able to anticipate a surge caused by a nuclear explosion," Ian said. "The Maeslantkering will fail! Without storm data, the computer won't know that a surge is coming, and the gates will be left wide open. The shock waves caused by the explosion will pummel through."

Ian was in such agony, he almost couldn't bear to ask the next question. "Where exactly is this computer-operated barrier?"

Cara frowned into her phone. "The Maeslantkering protects Rotterdam—which is about an hour's drive from here. Over half a million lives will be at risk— probably more, considering the holiday. With Rotterdam being the second-largest city in the Netherlands, people are most likely swarming there as well. Oh, and get this, Rotterdam's nickname is 'Gateway to Europe.'"

"I knew that capital G was important," Dan said, smacking his fist on the table, rattling all the china.

But Ian barely heard him. His head was pounding. His heart was racing. Over half a million lives at risk, and it fell on him to save them.

Dan couldn't move without slamming into another body. Horns blew in his ear and streamers flew overhead as Team A scrambled to find a taxi. But the streets were totally gridlocked. Even if they found an open cab, it would take forever to get out of Amsterdam. And it would take nearly as long to make it to a bus station or train depot with all the traffic.

"There has to be another way," Dan said, eyeing the only slightly less crowded canal flowing beneath a nearby bridge. "If we could, er, commandeer a boat . . . These canals, they lead out to the open ocean, don't they?" He pushed forward, blazing a trail between the throngs of people. Ian and Cara followed in his wake.

"That one?" Cara asked, pointing to a small aluminum boat moored against the side of the canal.

"Don't think that one's gonna cut it," Dan replied. "That one, on the other hand . . ." He cut close to the waterfront, pointing to a powerboat cruising downstream, not far from where they were walking. The powerboat had a narrow beam and a large outboard motor. "That one was built for speed."

The only problem was the driver. He was steering the high-performance vessel along at tortoise pace as he took in the sights and sounds of the celebration. "For the good of all," Dan said, "I just hope he can swim."

Catching an opening in the crowd, he sprinted forward, narrowing the distance between himself and the boat. Once he was right alongside it, he catapulted off the lip of the canal, over open water, and landed in the stern. Startled, the driver turned to face Dan as he charged the helm.

"Hey! This is a hijack. My friends and I need your boat!" Dan yelled over the cacophony of their surroundings.

The driver pushed back the sun flap on his hat and raised his fists, welcoming a fight.

"Dang," Dan said. "And I was hoping to do this the easy way." He wasn't far outsized—just a few inches shorter—but he was slightly out-footed by the driver. When the driver took a swing at Dan, his stance remained solid. When Dan ducked, he wobbled to the side and nearly fell overboard before regaining his balance.

I've got to go for the feet, he thought, realizing he knew how to fight.

Launching himself forward like a missile, he dove for the man's canvas loafers. The driver jumped to avoid the projectile headed straight for him, and when he did, Dan reached out and gave the man a little shove. That was all it took.

Dan watched over the side and was rewarded with a large splash. "Huh, that *was* easy. Thanks!" he called when the man's head popped back above the surface.

Then he whipped the boat around next to the wooden dock where Ian and Cara stood, wide-eyed and waiting.

"Jump!" Dan screamed. His friends took the plunge together. Dan hit the throttle as soon as their feet connected with the stern. The boat careened down the canal as Dan swerved to avoid the water taxis and catamarans trickling into the city through the webs of channels.

The last few years had trained Dan to be aware of his surroundings at all times—to always expect an ambush. So even though he was occupied with navigating the speeding boat, he didn't miss the lone figure standing on the bridge before them, drawing a small, shiny object from the pocket of his Windbreaker.

That the object was a weapon immediately registered in Dan's mind.

"Gunman!" Dan yelled to warn the others. "Dead ahead. We're going to pass right under him." There wasn't much cover to be found inside the boat, but Ian and Cara hit the deck and Dan practically hugged the dash panel as he ducked low and kept one hand on the wheel. His heart drummed in his chest as he steered the boat erratically.

A moving target is always harder to hit.

The boat veered left, then right, then left again as they approached the underpass.

As the boat neared the bridge, Dan couldn't stop himself from gazing up. He found himself staring down the barrel of a gun. He heard a pop and instantly his vision clouded with rainbow-colored particles. *This is it*, he thought. *I'm really dead this time. There's a tunnel with a light at the end and . . .*

Glitter?

The rainbow-colored particles shifting through the air were merely tiny pieces of shiny glitter. The gun had been a gag item, a not-so-funny joke, in Dan's opinion. The man who had shot at them wasn't some henchman sent by the Outcast. He was just some wise guy celebrating King's Day with a rainbow glitter gun.

As they exited the tunnel beneath the bridge and light assaulted his eyes, Dan glanced back at Cara and Ian sprawled across the bottom of the boat. Ian was shielding Cara with his body, and his back was blanketed by a thin film of glitter that glistened like minuscule gems in the sunlight.

"Um, guys?" Dan said.

Their eyes blinked open. Ian took one look at all the glitter and quickly clambered to his feet, allowing Cara to rise as well.

"Sorry. False alarm," Dan said.

"Clearly." Ian shook himself and brushed off the glitter. But when it was all gone, his shaking continued. The trembles seemed to embarrass Ian, and Dan looked away.

Throwing yourself between your friends and gunfire took remarkable bravery. Dan had no doubt that Ian was brave. But as Dan sped down the canal on the way toward violent, open seas and the threat of horrendous calamity, he worried that their leader was cracking under all the pressure.

CHAPTER 19

Mount Fuji, Japan

Nellie had never been so cold in all her life, and navigating in the whiteout was like walking around with a bucket on her head. She couldn't tell up from down, left from right. Even with the balaclava snug around her face, the wind buffeted her ears. Layers of clothing couldn't stop the icy chill from leaching all warmth from her body. Magnus was a pussycat compared to this storm.

Nellie had known they were in trouble the moment she and Sammy reemerged from the secret tunnel. One step into the blizzard—just one—and the world had slipped away, obscure and imperceptible through the raging swaths of wind and ice.

A second step and she'd realized that the situation could be fatal. And there was nothing more daunting than knowing they were up against a force as big and insidious as the cold.

She tugged on Sammy's coat sleeve to make him stop walking. If she lost connection, she'd never be able to find him in the whiteout. Sammy huddled close to her and his body gave off some heat, but not enough. A new plan was in order, but the cold was numbing her brain right along with all her senses.

Think, Gomez, she told herself, and focused her mind. Shelter was their number one priority. They'd never find their way down Mount Fuji through the blowing snow. The huts were all closed, and they'd die of hypothermia if they didn't find shelter from the elements soon.

No one, save Magnus and perhaps the restaurant owner, knew they were here, so a snowcat rescue was out of the question. And if no one was coming, and there wasn't shelter to be found, they'd just have to make their own.

She'd heard that snow is an excellent insulator.

"We need to dig a cave," Nellie said, leaning close to Sammy's ear so as to be heard over the blaring winds. Already, her lips felt numb and raw. Her muscles protested when she willed them to move, and her bones ached from the cold as she removed a light-weight avalanche shovel from her pack.

Sammy's eyes took longer than usual to register his understanding. Nellie worried that he was feeling the numbing effects of the cold, too.

But he followed her lead as she dropped to her hands and knees in a place where the snow had naturally drifted into a pile. Her head swam as she scooped and pushed the snow with her hands, mounding the drift higher. Disorientation was one of the first symptoms of hypothermia.

She was close to knife's edge herself, and she needed to know if Sammy was all right. "Did you bring a corncob pipe, and a button nose, and two eyes made out of coal?" Nellie yelled, her tongue feeling heavy and sluggish as she spoke. It wasn't a particularly clever joke, but Sammy's answer would be telling. Confusion was another symptom of hypothermia.

"Don't worry. I haven't lost all my senses yet," Sammy said, equally slowly. "And no, I don't have coal or a corncob pipe. But I have a synthetic thumb. It might work just as well as a button for the snowman's nose."

Nellie's face was too frozen to smile, but relief swept over her. *If only we were merely playing in the snow.*

The wind howled and blasted them with a fresh spray of ice. Nellie's eyelids and the tiny circle of exposed skin around her mouth stung in the frigid air. Their mound diminished in the wind.

Nellie waited until the gusts waned, then shouted, "Help me pack it down!" Sammy nodded and patted a clump of snow on top to hold the drift in place.

When they had a large, packed pile, Nellie used the shovel to carve into the side of it. Sammy labored to remove everything she dug out away from the opening. Together they hollowed a dome, and then Nellie cut a ventilation hole to the surface and they crawled inside.

Digging into her pack, Nellie pulled out extra gear to sit on, a tin survival candle, two canteens, and the greasy sack with the grilled cheese sandwiches they'd ordered from the restaurant. Then she used the pack to block the entrance.

"People pay decent money to stay in hotels made entirely of ice, you know," Nellie said. Her fingers were clumsy as she lit the candle and handed Sammy his sandwich. "Don't think I'm going to go to this extreme for all our dates," she teased.

Sammy smiled as he scooched closer to her and warmed both his hands and the sandwich over the flame. "It is rather romantic, other than the whole we-might-not-make-it-out-of-here-alive part."

"Yeah, that does put a damper on things, doesn't it?" Nellie said. "That and knowing that Magnus has probably broken out of the vault by now. I bet he's getting ready to hand over all the Tomas clues to the Outcast, and we can't do anything to stop him."

Nellie didn't know if it was heat from the candle or from her anger, but her face suddenly felt warmer. "Who knows how many of the clues the Outcast has already? I've got to warn my kiddos."

"Most blizzards last somewhere between four and ten hours," Sammy said. "Even if the storm does end soon, it's probably not safe to hike down at night. It's going to get even colder once the sun goes down."

"Colder" was unimaginable to Nellie at the moment. Even inside the relative warmth of the snow cave, her mind still felt dull and her extremities were numb.

"One way or the other, we should probably stay put until morning," Sammy continued.

Nellie didn't like it, but she conceded. "Okay, we'll wait until sunrise, assuming the sun breaks through the clouds. You said *most* last four to ten hours. How long *could* this blizzard last?"

Sammy dropped his gaze to the tiny flicker of the candle's flame. "Some blizzards last for days, sometimes even weeks," he said bleakly.

Nellie glanced at the candle, too. The tin said it had a six-hour burn time. Other than the warmth their bodies gave off, it was their only source of heat. "Let's just hope that this blizzard is short-lived, and that by some miracle we outlast the storm."

CHAPTER 20

Hook of Holland, the Netherlands

Dan wasn't prone to seasickness. Unfortunately, he couldn't say the same for his friends. Cara's face had a yellow-green tint to it, and Ian had lurched over the side of the speedboat and vomited three times in the distance between Amsterdam and the mouth of the Schenr River.

If there'd been time, Dan would've pulled the boat ashore to give them a break from the vigorous bouncing from one wave to the next. There wasn't time.

Dan swiveled his head to check on his passengers just as Ian wiped the corners of his mouth with a silk pocket square.

While Dan's attention was focused on the backseat, Ian's hand abruptly dropped to his lap and his jaw fell open. Dan's eyes shifted to Cara, who seemed every bit as awestruck.

When he turned his gaze back over the bow of the boat he saw what they were gaping at. Before them, the Maeslantkering was just coming into view. More than seven stories tall, the curved steel gates sat like a pair of slightly cockeyed parentheses on either side of the river. Behind the gates, triangular steel trusses expanded along the edge of the water for nearly seven hundred feet.

"We're supposed to move *those* things?" Dan croaked. The task that could save their lives and all of Rotterdam seemed utterly impossible now that he'd seen the barrier.

"No wonder Anki was so confident," Cara piped in. "Each arm of the Maeslantkering is as big as a real-life Eiffel Tower."

Ian moaned as the boat jerked against the top of a wave. "They're open, of course, and would you look at how many boats are on this side of the arms—the wrong side."

Dan reined in his feelings of hopelessness. Nothing was ever accomplished by giving up. "We'll just have to find a way to warn the boats—get them all to move into port before we shut the gates," Dan replied, though he had no idea how. Finding a place to dock their boat would probably be a good start. He cut back on the throttle and trawled the boat slowly into the Nieuwe Waterweg, the primary ship canal between Rotterdam and the sea.

As they passed through the open barrier, his eyes were naturally drawn to the Maeslantkering looming above them. From what he could tell, the doors of the

surge barrier were essentially gigantic platforms floating in man-made inlets next to the canal.

"The computer tells the doors to swing out into the
river, and a hydraulic system fills them with water.
The weight of the water sinks the floating arms and
then locks them into place," Cara said.

The water inside the channel was calmer, and Dan
was pleased to see that Cara's skin was returning to a
more natural hue. He nodded his head. Then he
searched the banks for an open slot, swerving the
boat into the first one he found.

Once he'd glided the boat into the slot, he hopped
out and hitched it to a post. He gave Ian and Cara
both a hand as they scrambled out after him and
onto shore.

Ian listed back and forth on the dock, having not
yet found his land legs. "We've got to find someone to
help us shut the gates," he sputtered. Then he planted
his feet and stabilized his legs with a hand on each
knee.

Dan's eyes darted from person to person, combing
the area for anyone with authority. What he saw
chilled him. It was nothing but moms and dads push-
ing strollers down the sidewalk, cyclists, and tourists
taking photos with their cameras.

His eyes finally rested on a small building with
aluminum siding just a short distance away. "There,"
he said, and read the words off the side of the
building:

Het Keringhuis
PUBLIEKSCENTRUM WATER

"*Publiekscentrum.* Public Center. It has to be some sort of visitor center. Perhaps we can find someone to help us there."

Ian rose to his full height and, having regained his balance, charged forward. The three of them raced down the sidewalk, past several flagpoles, and through the sliding glass doors of the visitor center.

A man with a ruddy beard and chin-length ginger hair was giving a guided tour to a group of ten just inside the door. "One of the busiest seaports in the world, Rotterdam is a vibrant, international city on the water with an impressively modern skyline," the tour guide said. "The Maeslantkering has allowed commerce to thrive in Rotterdam and at the same time offers a world-renowned level of flood protection."

Dan browsed the entryway and noticed two stacks of fliers beside the door. He passed over the stack with fireworks clip art at the top of each page and picked up a piece of paper displaying the artwork of two lions holding a shield beneath a golden crown.

Ian and Cara continued to move forward, but Dan froze in his tracks. The artwork on the flier he'd picked up represented the royal coat of arms of the

Netherlands. And what he read sent a shiver down his spine.

"Hold up." He whispered so as not to disturb the guided tour. He glanced at a digital clock sitting on top of a reception desk near the front of the room and then back down at the flier.

"Well?" Ian said impatiently.

Dan felt his face grow hot, his nerves tingling. He turned a wide-eyed gaze back on his friends. "We only have forty-one minutes until the nuke goes off."

Cara blanched. "What makes you say that?" she asked.

He pushed the flier beneath their noses. "This says King Willem-Alexander is touring cities across the Netherlands for King's Day. He's expected to make an appearance at Oude Haven, Rotterdam's historic old harbor, at noon today. It's 11:19 now." Dan gestured toward the clock.

" 'The Gateway floods when autonomy fails. The torrent erases the Dutch king's trail,' " Cara recited. She shook her head. "Oh, no!"

Dan's stomach revolted. The boat ride may not have made him sick, but the thought of the surge coming, and what little time they had left to stop it, did him in.

A storm seemed to be brewing inside Ian as well. He clenched his jaw and made a beeline for the tour guide, the only employee in sight.

"The tour is over," Ian announced to the sightseers. "Your lives are in danger. I suggest you find higher ground!" When the tour group just stood there, stunned, Ian added, "What is wrong with you people? Posthaste! You're all going to die if you don't listen to me." He clapped his hands at them. "Get out of here at once, I say!"

There were a few murmurs of surprise, followed by an older gentleman calling out, "Eh, what was that?"

"He said we're going to die if we don't leave," a younger man standing next to him answered in a decidedly skeptical tone.

"We're going to have pie when we leave?"

"No, *die*."

When the elderly man cupped his ear, the younger one rolled his eyes and shouted, "HE SAID WE'RE GOING TO DIE!"

"Humph. Well, I'd rather have cake," the old man grumbled.

"Let's just go, Dad," the younger man said. "We'll come back for a tour later—*after* we've replaced the battery in your hearing aid."

"Who said anything about lemonade? I said I want cake!"

Ian scuttled after the tour group, herding them like a little Welsh corgi snapping at the heels of live-stock. Then, momentarily looking quite pleased with himself, Ian tapped the bearded tour guide on the shoulder. "Not you. You are going to close the gates for me."

"I'm going to do what?"

"Are you deaf? I demand you shut the arms immediately! Close the Maeslantkering. I shouldn't have to chivy you along, too. Just do as I say!"

"I can't. What is going on here? Is this a practical joke?" The tour guide brightened and looked around. "Is someone filming me?"

"No, it's not a joke! I'm dead serious." Dan and Cara watched helplessly as Ian grew more flustered by the second. "We don't have time for incredulity, you twit. If you don't know how to shut the gates, find someone for me who does."

An unidentifiable expression flitted across the man's face and he began speaking in a low, pacifying voice. "You must understand, we only close the gates for testing once a year. You can come back at the end of September if you care to view the event. It really is quite impressive."

"I'm not a tourist!" Ian staggered on his feet. "Listen to me. In forty minutes, a powerful surge will breach the Maeslantkering unless you shut the gates." Ian took the man by the shoulders and began to shake a little too forcefully. "*You*. You can save Rotterdam."

The tour guide gave Ian a long, measuring glance, and then nodded his head. "You're right," he said slowly. "I probably should make a phone call. If you'll just excuse me for a moment . . ." He cautiously took one step back, then another, and then he turned and bolted.

"What did I say?" A pained and utterly flummoxed look crossed Ian's face. "This is impossible," he lamented before chasing after the man. "Wait a minute. Exactly whom are you calling?" he shouted. "I demand you tell me at once!"

Cara began to follow, but Dan grabbed her by the arm. "There has to be another way." He scanned the visitor center, taking in the sight of a tiny replica of the Delta Works, which included a scale model of the Maeslantkering, and then all the black-and-white photos hanging on the walls, cataloging the North Sea flood of 1953.

He wished like mad that his sister were there. Amy would have a solution to this mess, or at least be able to talk Ian into getting his head back in the game. Dan could hear him pounding on a door. The tour guide must have locked himself in a room at the back of the center.

With both Ian and Amy out of the picture, Dan knew it fell on him to make the hard decisions. And that was like being handed a giant lead ball and being told not to drop it. He inhaled deeply and continued to canvass the room. His gaze flicked from the clock, as another minute ticked away, to the desktop computer situated next to it on the reception desk.

"That's it!" Dan cried. Ian's flip-out had created the perfect diversion. "Cara, there's a computer and no one to stop you. It might be tied to the same network as the computer that controls the surge barrier. Do you think you can crack it?"

Cara perked up. "What do you have in mind?"

"You tell me. There must be a way to trick the computer into triggering a closure. You said it ran on algebra or something."

"On an algorithm."

"Right! Can't you feed it false data or something? Make it think there's a storm raging outside even though it's bright and sunny?"

"Maybe. Or I might be able to change the parameters altogether. I'll figure out something," Cara said, a confident smile blooming on her face. "As long as Ian keeps the guide occupied."

Just then, Ian's voice came screeching from the back of the visitor center. "By *security*, I do hope you mean the naval forces!"

"No worries there," Dan said, and they both sprang into action. As Cara slid into place behind the keyboard, Dan made a mad dash for the sliding doors. Beyond the glass, he caught a glimpse of a pontoon boat lingering outside the gates of the barrier. A family was laughing and barbecuing onboard, out for a leisurely day on the water.

"Where are you going?" Cara called.

"I have to find a way to warn the ships."

CHAPTER 21

Nieuwe Waterweg, the Netherlands

If Dan was going to die today, at least he'd go out with a bang.

He snagged a flier from the other stack as he fled the visitor center.

The fireworks on it had caught his attention before, but, as with any disaster, things had to be taken one step at a time. Now that Cara, he hoped, was on her way to activating the gates, Dan could focus on clearing the busy waterway.

The text beneath the image of fireworks exploding in the sky was written entirely in Dutch. Dan flipped the flier over.

Dan liked fireworks every bit as well as the next thirteen-year-old, but it was the last line that got him really excited.

If there were plans to restrict shipping traffic, then he was betting that at least some of the larger, slower-moving ships had been given prior notification. If he could somehow set off the fireworks early, perhaps it would alert the cargo-ship captains, and they'd start bringing their boats into port. And if the big guys were moving in, Dan imagined that all the little tugs, fishing boats, and pontoons would follow.

Nervously grinding his teeth, he searched the waterway. The barbecuing family was puttering farther out to sea. He inhaled sharply. Admittedly, his fireworks plan was a long shot, but he had to try something.

Pulling out his cell phone, Dan noticed that five more minutes had vaporized. He set an alarm for noon and the countdown began.

35 minutes.

Dan's chest tightened. *If I were a fireworks shell, where would I be?* he asked himself as he surveyed the grounds outside the visitor center.

It was hard not to notice all the people still streaming down the sidewalk. And who could blame them? It was a bright, sunny day *and* a national holiday, after all. If Dan wasn't a Cahill, he'd be doing the same exact thing.

The old adage that "ignorance is bliss" popped into his brain. But he couldn't entirely swallow the thought. If a fight for his life was coming down the pipeline, he'd want to know. He'd want to be able to do something.

A woman wearing a vibrant orange dress and carrying a saxophone case beneath her arm caught his eye.

" 'Live band,' " Dan said musingly. Perhaps this woman was one of the musicians playing "Het Wilhelmus" during the fireworks display. He did his best to dissolve into the background. Then, merging with the pedestrian traffic, he silently followed the saxophone player down the sidewalk.

Find the band, find the fireworks.

He trailed the musician for a block and a half before the woman stopped at a shady spot alongside the canal. Then she flipped open her case on the ground and pulled out a shiny brass instrument. After placing a cardboard sign that read TIPS on the concrete in front of her, she began playing.

Dan silently cursed himself for wasting time.

30 minutes.

Time was ticking away and he was no closer to finding the shells. Despairingly, he spun on his heel, looking for any sign of where the fireworks might be. It was then that he noticed a small hill just beyond the visitor center.

Considering that so much of the land was well below sea level, high points were pretty scarce. The hill might just be the perfect place to set up the display. Dan squinted. Through the people and trees, Dan could almost make out a row of rudimentary plywood frames, plastic tubes, and jumbles of wire. They looked like the type of makeshift materials that shells could be launched from. His feet pounded the pavement again, this time at full speed.

A chain-link fence encircled the hillside. As Dan drew near he took a running leap. Lodging his sneakers between the links, he scrambled the remaining distance to the top, then hurled his body over the side.

25 minutes.

He sprinted for the apex.

At the highest point he found endless rows of steel tubes, supported by sand and wooden racks spread out before him. The tubes were locked in firing position. Wires ran like blood-filled veins from each tube to separate circuit boards attached to each rack.

When Dan dashed to the first circuit board, he found a cable running from it to a tangle of other cables leading away from their corresponding boards.

It reminded him of the webs of canals in Amsterdam: branching out and flowing in a multitude of directions, but all originating at a single source. The canals all led back to the sea. Dan was guessing that the cables led to some sort of firing mechanism. All he had to do was follow the line of cables.

He tracked the twist of cables to a steel blast shield. Behind it sat the main firing control panel. Hope tugged at him as he tried to make heads or tails of all the buttons. He just had to figure out how to turn the panel on, and then he'd let the shells rip.

"Wie bent U? Stoppen!" someone yelled.

Dan glanced up to see an irate man in a hard hat running toward him from a panel truck parked just over the ridge of the hill. "Whoa, take it easy," Dan said, raising his hands and acting like he wasn't just about to press every button on the panel.

"Get away from there!" the man said, switching from Dutch to English. He was only about ten feet from the fireworks pods and closing the gap between them quickly.

Dan's eyes darted to the man's hard hat and then back to the firing panel. "Sorry I have to do this to you, dude." He dove behind the blast wall. As fast as his fingers could operate, he threw the switches.

"DUCK!" Dan screamed right before the first shell erupted from its steel tube. It made a hollow *phruump* sound as it left the cannon, a *swishhhh* as it rocketed into the sky, followed by sizzles and crackles, then *BANG!* as it discharged directly overhead.

Then it happened over and over again in rapid succession—grand finale times ten.

The sound was deafening, painful almost, as it rattled inside him. The air popped. Smoke and sparks engulfed the hillside. Dan's eyes burned and he choked on the thick gray clouds. Being this close was like being stuck in a war zone with explosives detonating all around him. It was electrifying and scary. And he hoped it worked.

At some point he'd switched from pressing buttons to using his hands as earmuffs. With his ears still covered, and with gunpowder and sparkles still bursting in the sky, he peeked out from behind the blast wall.

The man was flat on the ground, using his arms for added protection over the hard hat. But he was slowly inching forward, army crawling his way toward Dan.

20 minutes.

Dan dropped his hands from his ears and slid the panel off his lap. He'd just deployed twenty minutes' worth of fireworks in less than a minute. If that hadn't been enough to draw the ships into the harbor, he wasn't sure what would.

Before the man could grab hold of him, Dan jumped to his feet and tore down the hillside. As he raced back toward the fence, he could see a cargo ship moving through the gates, and the family's pontoon boat behind it.

"Yes!" he screamed, and fist-pumped at the sky.

He could also see that the crescent-shaped buoyant arms of the Maeslantkering were entering the waterway. He fist-pumped the sky a second time. Cara had hacked the computer and the gates were closing. Still, as they inched toward each other, he was aware of the tick of the clock. The gates were moving so slowly. What if they didn't shut in time? Then he caught sight of something that caused his stomach to leap into his throat. Just beyond the arms of the barrier, in the mouth of the Schenr River, a small fishing boat was having engine trouble.

The boat was dead in the water.

CHAPTER 22

Nieuwe Waterweg, the Netherlands

15 minutes to detonation.

Don't think, just act, Dan told himself. If he let what could happen sink in—that heading out on the waterway meant he might not come back—he'd never do what needed to be done. So he gave in to instinct.

He charged for the stolen speedboat left docked along the riverside. His motions were deft and sure as he untied the boat and jumped aboard.

12 minutes.

The engine hummed to life when Dan started the ignition and roared when he hit the throttle. Once again, he raced against traffic as he wound his way out to the sea.

10 minutes.

As he neared the shutting arms, an oil tanker blocked his way. Dan veered around it, cutting dangerously close to the ship's stern as he slipped the speedboat between the tanker and the gates.

The captain of the boat laid on the horn.

8 minutes.

Dan ignored the blare ringing in his ears. He ignored the ocean spray wetting his cheeks and the jarring bounce of the boat on the waves as he sped into open water. He only cared about one thing: getting to the fishing boat before the surge came.

6 minutes.

When he closed in on the small vessel, Dan saw a fisherman leaning over the back of the boat, messing with the outboard motor. The motor was smoking and sputtering in the water but refused to turn over. A second fisherman stood at the helm, barking orders to the man tinkering with the engine.

4 minutes.

Cutting the ignition, Dan drifted up beside them. However, he couldn't halt the wake, and the fishermen's boat jostled in the water. They quickly flashed him angry glares, then ignored him entirely.

Dan forced his face muscles into a smile. Panic caused people to behave in unpredictable ways. No need to further upset the fishermen if he didn't have to.

3 minutes.

"Hi there!" Dan said, keeping his tone cheerful even though fear was running his insides through a meat grinder. The two kept their attention focused on the malfunctioning motor. "Looks like you're having some trouble. Can I give you a lift?" Dan offered.

"Nee!" the man behind the wheel shouted back at him. Without so much as another glance in Dan's direction, the fisherman waved him off.

2 minutes.

"Look. You've got to come with me now," Dan said, still trying to play it cool. Then he added under his breath, "The sea is about to get super turbulent." A few waves, small in comparison to the ones he knew were coming, rocked the boat. The fishermen didn't move.

They had just precious seconds left. Dan didn't want to waste the last moments of his life bickering with strangers. And his panic was making it difficult to concentrate on the task at hand. His knees felt weak as he contemplated his next move.

1 minute.

"Seriously, dudes, I don't want to leave without you. If you're coming, we need to get out of here, like, *pronto*," Dan said a bit more forcefully. "The gates are almost closed, and trust me, we don't want to be on this side when they lock into place."

Something about the quaver in Dan's voice must have finally piqued the fishermen's interest. They both stopped what they were doing and glanced up. The younger of the two looked past Dan. Eyes widening, and mouth flopping open, he pointed at the moving gates of the surge barrier.

Noon.

The North Sea erupted.

The air cracked and tingled before the *boom* reached Dan's ears. Absolutely everything shuddered as an enormous fist of water thrust its way forth from the sea. Although it was hundreds of feet away, Dan could feel the underwater explosion inside his chest. He tasted salt and smelled the dank, moist air as the line between water and sky blurred.

The fishermen's heads swiveled on their necks. Their faces registered every bit of shock Dan was feeling. Behind a ring of dark water, a plume rose higher and higher in the heavens, building up and out, until it hung like an ominous cauliflower-shaped cloud thousands of feet in the air.

It was just like the videos he'd watched, and Dan knew that no force was strong enough to fight gravity forever. The base surge of water droplets would reach them first. But then a hollow column of water rising within the plume would fall, crashing and tangling as it again met the sea. All the compression and expansion would cause a rising swell. A series of powerful and destructive waves would follow. Dan's gut was ice. "GO!" he shrieked.

The men launched themselves from one vessel to the next just as a small wave rocked Dan's boat and pushed it a slight distance.

The first man caught one hand on the gunwale cleat and heaved himself up out of the water and into the boat. The second lost his grip and was dunked under by the starboard side. Dan plunged both hands deep into the chilly water, locking them around the flailing man's wrists, as a spray of water blasted him in the face.

On the horizon the enormous column began its descent. As it fell, the column displaced the water beneath it. The result was a circular, ring-shaped wall, dispelled in all directions. It would overcome them in a matter of seconds, taking the powerboat into its fold and sweeping it to the bottom of the sea.

As soon as he'd yanked the second man into the boat, Dan flipped the key over in the ignition. The boat revved to life and Dan spun the bow around so that it pointed directly at the narrowing gap between the closing gates.

The mist created by the surge caught up to them. Rain pelted Dan's skin and blurred his vision. He didn't dare turn to look, but he sensed the wall of water bearing down on the motor. A giant wave was on their tail. The stern of the boat pitched upward in the water just as Dan bore down on the throttle. There was a moment of weightlessness. Then, instead of being pulled to the depths, the motor propelled them upward until they were riding just beneath the swell of the immense wave.

Dan felt like a fly on the back of a storming beast. He felt tiny and powerless. They were hurtling toward the closing gates, unable to stop now even if they wanted to. A new fear rose inside him. They were going to be crushed against the enormous, clamping arms.

The fishermen hollered at him in Dutch. Roaring waves, thundering rain, and the sound of his thumping heart muted their words. But despite the background noise and the language barrier, he could tell by the lilt in their voices that they were hysterical.

The unshaven fisherman moved forward in the jouncing boat. He grabbed Dan by the shoulder, then gestured wildly at the Maeslantkering. *"Nee! Nee! De Poorten!"*

"It's okay, we're going to make it," Dan said, knowing full well that, more than anything, he was trying to convince himself. The gap between the curved steel walls already looked way too small, and they were still thirty . . . twenty . . . a mere ten feet away. "Hold on!" he shouted.

Dan shut his eyes and cranked a hard left on the steering wheel. The speedboat tipped sharply in the direction he'd turned, skimming the water on the port side only.

The belly of the boat scraped against the steel arm with a terrible *screeeeeeeech!*

Dan could hear the windshield shatter, and he ducked down and braced himself as shards of glass flew overhead. The earsplitting gnash and grate of metal on metal was nearly unbearable as the gates clipped the motor and it died.

A loud *BANG* resounded in the air and the boat plummeted as it rolled off the crest of the wave and fell into the canal. Dan's eyes whipped open as he and the two men were thrown from the boat and plunged toward the water. They splashed down hard, and for a second Dan's world was nothing but a cold rush of dark and white water. He kicked and struggled against the river, his lungs constricting, until his head broke the surface. One fisherman popped up next to him, and then an agonizing few seconds later, the other one did, too.

They were both sheet white—like two wet ghosts—as the current pushed the three of them and the boat downstream.

Behind them, the arms of the Maeslantkering were rapidly filling with water and sinking into place. The bang they'd heard was the sound of the gates locking shut.

Dan braced himself for the onslaught of waves. When nothing more than a harmless spray sloshed over the top of the barrier, he nearly choked with relief. The tsunami had been held at bay, and Team A was to thank.

CHAPTER 23

Airspace above Nieuwe Waterweg, the Netherlands

"Did it ever occur to you to shower before picking me up?" the Outcast sneered. He wasn't fond of spending time in close quarters with Magnus Hansen—even when personal hygiene wasn't in question. However, he was fond of killing two birds with one stone.

Magnus was piloting the Outcast's helicopter, and the bag containing the Clues that Magnus had stolen rested at the Outcast's feet. And, thanks to the helicopter's domed windows, the Outcast had just been treated to a glorious front-row viewing of all the excitement in the Nieuwe Waterweg.

The column that had risen from the sea had been tremendous. The wall of water it had driven toward the canal was horrifyingly grand. And Dan's gallant race to bring the fishermen safely into harbor before the gates closed had been a real nail-biter.

Grace would have been proud of her grandson. *But not of me*, the Outcast thought. Resentment churned in his stomach. Long after her death, Grace's opinion of him still mattered. Her judgment ate at him like acid.

He'd always been able to charm his way into people's hearts. He'd identified their weaknesses, silently prodded their brittlest places until they snapped. *That's how you gain control.*

It was simple enough. People needed direction. Whether they knew it or not, they yearned to be dominated. But when he'd pulled back the veneer and revealed his tactics to the one person whose love actually counted, he'd been rejected. It haunted him still.

In their early years, there'd been a synchrony to his and Grace's actions that everyone envied. Their hopes and ideals had been the same. It was merely their differing styles of execution that got in the way.

The Outcast felt a twang of longing for what could have been. Grace here beside him, watching their grandson's valiant efforts. Discussing how best to mold the boy. Courage and tenacity were in Dan's DNA. So was a penchant for corruptibility.

If Grace had only understood the bigger picture, they could have built a legacy together. But she'd never been able to get past the destruction, the tearing down of ideas and people, the tactical deceit necessary to diminish, and then the final caress that reshaped minds and futures. The Outcast was erecting something better, something stronger than any Cahill had ever known. But first he had to break the Cahill family, and then the world.

As for whether or not the Netherlands ever met devastation to rival that of Hurricane Katrina's, the Outcast had never truly cared. What he wanted was chaos, and that's what he got. While others succumbed to the fear he caused and the disorder around them, he would gain control.

As Magnus flew the chopper away from the waterway they met a search and rescue helicopter headed the opposite direction. The Outcast waved.

The pilot did not wave back. He was terror-stricken—just one more person looking for a way to find meaning in senseless tragedy. It was beautiful.

The Outcast would show them the way.

Magnus flipped on the helicopter's radio and the Outcast listened attentively as news reports began to trickle in. The unsuspecting people of the Netherlands were reeling. They didn't know what had hit them and could only speculate how much worse it would've been if the Maeslantkering hadn't closed. Little did they know, they were merely disposable chess pieces in the greatest game ever played.

And despite the fact that his third disaster had been stopped, the Outcast was one step closer to checkmate.

CHAPTER 24

Video Conference, Various Locations

As Dan gave the blow-by-blow on how he'd escaped the surge just as the gates clamped shut, Amy's heart cramped in her chest. Her breath hitched in her throat, and she touched the computer screen his face appeared on. It was agonizing to know how close he'd come to death, but knowing how well he'd handled it made her ache with pride.

"Yo, tell them about me!" Jonah chimed in from where he was propped up on the hotel bed.

Amy recounted their run-in with Alek Spasky. "Forty stiches," she said. Then a wry smile played on her lips. "Someone at the hospital leaked the story. Now there's all this speculation in the media that he was attacked by some wacked-out fan with a twisted obsession."

"Yeah. Completely took the heat off me for the Shakespeare madness. Earned me a bunch of sympathy instead!" Jonah's voice was gleeful. "Oh, and show them what you found."

Amy rifled through a folder and then held up a photo of a handsome young man wearing a dark suit with a skinny black tie and horn-rimmed glasses. There was an unsettling shrewdness in his eye. He had Amy's round cheeks and light brown hair. She found the resemblance distressing. "It's a photograph of Nathaniel Hartford—from about fifty years ago, I think," she said. "I found it in Grace's black files, along with some . . . other stuff."

Amy glanced down and to the right when she said "stuff." She'd wait until they had privacy to tell Dan the rest. "Ham's going to run an age progression on the photo for us now," she said. Ham sat down at the laptop.

Part of Amy wanted confirmation that Nathaniel was the Outcast, so they could move ahead. But a larger part of her hoped it wasn't him.

A few minutes later, Hamilton projected an image on both of their screens of an elderly man with modern-day glasses. Amy studied it and then shook her head. "I can't tell. The Outcast has had some work done. Can you take off the glasses? And give him a face lift or something?"

Ian piped up from the background. "Also, teeth whitening, Botox, laser resurfacing, collagen treatments . . . oh, and eyelid surgery to correct the sagging, I believe." After a moment of awkward silence, Ian added, "What? So I know a thing or two about plastic surgery. My mother went under the knife at each and every opportunity."

"Right," Ham said, and went back to work. The image he projected next resembled the first, but with night-and-day differences.

"It's like looking at 'before' and 'after' photos of models who've been Photoshopped," Dan said. "Not that I've been looking at pictures of models or anything," he added quickly, face reddening.

"That's our man," Amy said solemnly as Ham stood up, and she dropped back into the seat behind the computer. "The Outcast is Nathaniel Hartford—our grandfather." Quiet again fell over the bunch.

Amy was about to wrap things up and give them all time to let the revelation sink in, when a call popped up on the screen. "Nellie!"

Amy hit the green button, then the screen split in half and Nellie's face appeared next to Dan's. Saladin hopped on the desk, purring and rubbing against the screen until Amy gently nudged him aside.

"Kiddos!" Nellie squealed. Her eyes were alight and her smile was warm, but the bruises on her forehead, the blisters on her lips, and the chapped skin on her cheeks were more than a little alarming.

She was in some sort of café, Sammy beside her, and there were Japanese characters on the wall. A balaclava was pushed back on her head, and they appeared to be wearing layers of outerwear.

"Nellie?" Amy wondered. "Where were you?"

"Trapped in an ice cave for two days, but never mind," Nellie replied. "What matters is that you know what the Outcast is really after. These disasters are all just a diversion. His endgame is the clues," she said gravely. "And I know for a fact he has all the Tomas clues already."

Amy clenched her fists, digging her nails into her palms. It was as bad as she'd suspected. People were dying and places were being destroyed all so her grandfather could get his hands on the serum. It was messed up. It was sickening. And she'd had enough.

Amy scrutinized Dan's face on the computer screen, looking for any signs that he was ready to call it quits again. Ever since Grace had passed away, it seemed as though the world had done its best to break them both.

Knowing what they knew now—that the Outcast was their very own grandfather and that he'd stop at nothing to get the Clues—meant that things were only going to get worse. The decisions were going to be harder. Their actions would have even greater consequences as they grew older. Grace's files, heavy as a concrete block where they sat on her lap, were a heartbreaking reminder of that.

But Dan's face gazing back at her was unflinching. His jaw was hard set and determined. The look in his eyes reminded her how strong they both were. They were ready to take on whatever the Outcast threw at them next.

Amy felt confidence ballooning inside her. "Put Ian on," she said.

Dan stood up and moved out of view, and Ian's face appeared before her. Ian was a wilted version of his former self. His hair was unbrushed, his shirt had a tear in it, and his shoulders were slumped. There was barely an ounce of the Kabra arrogance left in him. Amy felt a twinge of guilt for ever having asked him to step into her role. It would surely be a knock-out blow if she asked him to step down.

"How are you holding up?" Amy asked gently.

"I feel like a perfect fool, if you really want to know."

Amy held her tongue. Anything she could say would only make things worse.

"That plonker at the visitor center refused to listen to reason. I don't know," Ian said. Amy detected a quaver in his voice. He tried to clear it before going on. "I thought being head of the Cahill family was going to be different, somehow. I thought people would recognize my authority and heed my demands. Instead, I have to take responsibility for every last thing that goes wrong, and let me tell you, loads of things go wrong in this family. You have no idea how many complaints I've had to listen to these past few months."

The expression on Ian's face changed. He spoke in a falsetto voice, "'Ian, why did you spend so much on tailoring your clothes this month? That money would've been better spent on a remodel of the Paris headquarters.' Or, this one was rich," he continued. "'Ian, the plumbing inside the Venice stronghold is on the fritz again.'" Ian shook his head disdainfully. "Why do they think they can come to me with every little loo problem? I tell you, I'd much rather be the one complaining than the one listening to all the complaints."

"Okay," Amy said in a precise and even tone.

"Okay?"

"Yes, it's okay." Amy held Ian's gaze. "If you don't want to listen to any more complaints, then you don't have to."

"I-I don't?" Ian stammered. "You mean I can just shut them up somehow? How does one go about shutting up dissenters?" His eyes widened with hope. "Are you suggesting that I use threats, poison—blackmail, perhaps!—to keep the peace?"

Amy scrunched her face in consternation. Getting through to Ian was even more difficult than she'd thought it would be. "No, Ian, I'm not. I'm saying that if you don't want to be the one with the responsibility anymore, if you don't want to be the person the Cahills turn to when they register their complaints, then you don't have to be. That's okay with Dan and me."

"Oh," Ian said quietly. "Oh, I see."

"You've done a terrific job, but if you want—"

"No, no, I understand. I understand perfectly now." Ian's shoulders began to quake and short puffs of air escaped through his nose.

"Ian, I'm so sorry. Don't cry. Dan and I . . . we just—" A great honking noise interrupted her. "Wait? Are you laughing?"

Ian threw back his head and did a very un-Ian-like thing. He whooped with joy. "Cry? Are you serious?"

He whooped again. "It's yours! All of it. Every last problem, every complaint and disaster—they're all yours, and Dan's, of course. Brilliant! Dan, get back in here! Your sister has something to tell you!"

Ian sprang from his seat, giving Amy a clearer view of the hotel room. Cara was standing by a window. When Ian ran to her, arms open, she beamed with delight, grabbed his cheeks, and planted a kiss firmly on his lips. He dipped her low and kissed her deeper.

"Gross! Cut that out!" Dan yelled.

He gagged loud enough for Amy to hear as he slid back in front of the screen. "Ian took that well, didn't he?" he asked his sister.

"Remarkably."

"So I guess this means it's up to us to stop the Outcast," Dan said. "I mean, I know we'll have help— our friends aren't going to ditch us. But it's you and me. We're the leaders again, right?"

"Right." Ian's outburst had offered a short reprieve from the seriousness of their predicament, but Amy felt the enormity of it come rushing back. Ian was right. Being in charge wasn't all it was cracked up to be. Being a leader meant being stuck with the hard choices and difficulties. It also meant being constantly tempted by all that power, the way Grace had been.

Per usual, Dan seemed to be reading her thoughts. "You know, I think we've actually done a pretty good job. Grace and Nathaniel"—her brother shook his head—"we're light-years ahead of our grandparents.

And don't even get me started on the previous generation of Kabras. Compared to the Cahill leaders that came before us, we're killing it!"

"Killing it?"

"You know what I mean. Our family may be the most powerful one in history, but we're a real mess. Seriously, we put the Mafia to shame."

Amy cracked a smile. "Some of our ancestors *were* in the Mafia."

"But not you and me. Through all our ups and downs, we've stayed solid. Sure, we've both thrown in the towel a time or two, but we always came back. This is what we were born to do."

Amy agreed. "I know. It feels natural now."

"And we have something that the leaders before us didn't have."

"What's that?"

"We have each other."

Amy's heart swelled. "Definitely. You didn't do so shabby on your own in the Netherlands, did you, dweeb? Sounds like you basically saved the day in Rotterdam."

Dan sat up a hair straighter in his chair. "Then that settles it. We're officially back in the saddle."

"For sure. But one thing has to change," Amy said. She leaned forward. "We've always played catch-up. We've always chased after the bad guys and followed a path that bad guys created. That has to stop. We can't sit around just waiting for the Outcast to spring the fourth disaster."

"So what do we do?" Dan asked. "Are we going to attack him, like Ian said?"

"No. We know who he is. We know what he wants. We *have* what he wants. We're going to set a trap."

As a grin spread across her brother's face, Amy inhaled sharply. She'd only just realized what setting a trap would mean. They had what the Outcast wanted, because all 39 Clues were stuck inside Dan's fortress of a head. To set a trap they would need bait.

And that bait would have to be Dan.